EARTH DIVIDED

Centuries had passed by on Earth since the Golden Amazon, Abna and Viona—the original Cosmic Crusaders—had set off on their interstellar quest. Their adventures had led them to travel in time, and their breaking of the light-barrier had also added to the time discrepancy between themselves and the Earth they had left. The science on Earth had advanced, not least because of the foundations the Crusaders themselves had laid. Now that advanced science reaches out to the depths of the galaxy, and snatches them back to a divided Earth. One half is in thrall to the 'Pagans,' scientific barbarians, who are seeking to overwhelm the remaining 'Normals'…unless the Crusaders can prevent the spread of scientific barbarism!

Another action-packed scientific adventure in the on-going saga of the Golden Amazon!

THE GOLDEN AMAZON SAGA

EARTH DIVIDED

THE GOLDEN AMAZON SAGA, BOOK 20

JOHN RUSSELL FEARN

Edited by Philip Harbottle

WILDSIDE PRESS

To the memory of Gwen Cowley

EARTH DIVIDED

CONTENTS

THE GOLDEN AMAZON SERIES

by Philip Harbottle

Earth Divided was the second 'Golden Amazon' novel to be published posthumously, after author John Russell Fearn's death in September 1960. It appeared in the 24th June 1961 issue of the Toronto *Star Weekly*—but had it not been for the courage and devotion of Fearn's widow, Carrie Fearn, it might never have appeared at all.

Carrie Fearn had been at her husband's side when he had suddenly collapsed in a Blackpool Church on 18 September, 1960. He was rushed to hospital in an ambulance, but was pronounced dead on arrival. The shock to his widow was devastating. Her own first husband, Blackpool businessman and holiday tour operator Billy Worth, had died as recently as 1955. Marrying Fearn—a long-time friend of the family—in November 1956, she had yet to complete her fourth wedding anniversary. A terribly short time—and now cruel fate had snatched away her second husband.

In her grief, she fell terribly ill herself, and for two weeks she struggled to recover. When she did so, she had to mentally steel herself to enter the room Fearn used as a study. The poignant memories it evoked threatened to overwhelm her, but she managed to overcome them and to search for the mss of novel she had known her husband was working on. She discovered that Fearn had been engaged in writing a new Amazon novel, *Earth Divided*. The pages of the mss were still on his desk, alongside his typewriter.

At first, it looked as if the mss was unfinished. What Mrs. Fearn had found was the first 117 pages of Fearn's *second*, polished version. But later she discovered another mss, which was the uncorrected *first draft* of a *completed* novel. Despite her grief, his widow had then retyped the remaining 25 pages. Naturally, she followed his exact wording, correcting only the spelling mistakes. Fortunately Fearn had been on good form whilst writing his draft, so there was no noticeable drop in quality—although Fearn would undoubtedly have tightened it had he lived to complete his final revision.

Her submission letter to Gwen Cowley was dated November 1960, and ran:

Dear Miss Cowley,

Very many thanks for your letter of 11 October, also thank you for your most kind sympathy in my so tragic loss.

I am sending you my husband's last Amazon story for your consideration. The last 25 pages I have typed myself from the rough draft. I trust I have done it all right. I don't know how many words should be on each page, but I trust that you will forgive and understand if I have not got the number quite right.

I did mention in my letter that I thought the last part of the story was in synopsis form, but on looking again, I find that what I thought was synopsis was the outline of this story, and also for the next Amazon story which he had hoped to follow on after this one. So this story is complete.

A sincere thank you Miss Cowley for letting me send this, his last story along, for I am very sure my husband would have wished me to try and do this for him.

My best wishes to you, always.

Yours very sincerely

Mrs. John Russell Fearn

Editor Gwen Cowley's practice was to have all submissions read first by assistants. The mss was then passed to her for a final decision, along with a memorandum of detailed comments and recommendations by the assistant.

As a regular contributor, the *Star Weekly* kept a file on Fearn, and the surviving letters from it are nowadays part of my personal Fearn Archive, from which I have already quoted. The detailed final editorial assessment sheet of EARTH DIVIDED has also survived, and makes fascinating reading. Gwen Cowley's detailed analysis of the story was dated January 23, 1961, and opened thusly:

> Last science fiction written by John Russell Fearn, who died last September. I think we should use this, as it is his last, and readers have sent in many letters asking if we will have another—also if we will have more. There won't be any more John Russell Fearn's, but he has had a tremendous following...

The two-page assessment ended:

> ...Fantastic but interesting reading for those who like science fiction, and there seem to be a lot of people who do.

Gwen Cowley then wrote to Mrs. Fearn on January 27, 1961, formally accepting the story. It eventually appeared in print in the June 24th issue of the *Star Weekly*.

The printed version was editorially abridged, losing some 10,000 words in the process.

After Mrs. Fearn died in 1982 and I was given access to Fearn's study by her Executors, I discovered the 34,000-words carbon copy version of the novel. This is the version that appears here, uncut.

CHAPTER 1

Cosmic Abduction

Untold light-centuries away from Earth, in the depths of the Milky Way Galaxy, the giant space-machine Ultra was drifting—or at least it seemed to be compared to the colossal speed to which it could attain on occasions… But the strange thing was that the Ultra was not alone in the vast reaches of infinite space. There was another Ultra no more than a million miles distant—gray, huge, and invincible. And with the passage of time they came nearer and nearer to each other. There was only one distinguishing difference—an enormous metal-scar, relic of one of the many battles in which the genuine Ultra had been involved, whereas there was no such evidence on the duplicate. But that the two machines were otherwise identical there was no doubt.

Within the battle-scarred Ultra, the Golden Amazon, leader of the famed interstellar Cosmic Crusaders, was distinctly puzzled—which in itself was remarkable for there were few problems which baffled this beautiful superwoman of Earth with her incredible mastery of science and its varied implications. She stood now alone in the control room, as poised and curvaceous as a young goddess, her head thrown back as she stared through the observation window, her masses of golden hair tumbling down to her shoulders.

At a slight sound she suddenly turned. The control room door slid back to admit Abna, her husband, a seven-foot blond giant who claimed massive Jupiter as his birthplace. He came forward, questions in his smiling blue eyes.

"Solved it yet?" he asked, stopping by the window—and the Amazon shook her head.

"Not yet, I've been thinking about it, but I haven't done anything very practical like analysis tests, to confirm or contradict the theory that it may be only a spatial mirage."

Abna looked at the distant second Ultra, clear as a gray ovoid against the absolute black of space. Then he shook his head.

"No, Vi, that isn't a mirage—even though I grant you that they can exist in space as easily as on a planet. It's a ship all right—and what's more it's a duplicate of our own. Whether that is coincidence or deliberate I can't say. Only way is to go to it and find out."

"In that I agree, but we ought to know first that we're not chasing rainbows."

With that the Amazon moved swiftly to the assembly of instruments near the control panel. Switches clicked beneath her yellow fingers until finally she was surveying an array of dials, which gave her a cross-sectional reading, electronically, of the spaceship in the distance. Abna came across from the window and joined her.

"Well, there you are," he said finally. "Nothing of the mirage about that. It exists all right—"

"Distance half a million miles and made of various metals amongst which the most predominant is transite steel…" The Amazon's voice trailed off and she stood thinking, a sharp light in her violet eyes.

"What's the trouble now?" Abna asked.

"No trouble—just an interesting thought." The Amazon waved a hand to the dials. "In the analysis of the machine's composition our readings show that all the metals concerned are Earthly—except a few which could have been discovered since we left the Earth. Transite is definitely an Earth-metal—about 15 times tougher than tungsten."

A slight surprise registered on Abna's handsome face.

"Which suggests," the Amazon concluded, switching off, "that the machine is Earthly in origin, but what it's doing way out here in the Milky Way is a mystery. Also, why is it designed to look exactly like this Ultra of ours— except for the metal scar on the prow which we have and that one hasn't."

There was silence for a moment as they both considered the problem. It was broken as two lithe young women stepped into the control room, followed by a young man with very broad shoulders. Viona, daughter of the Amazon, and Thania—teenager of a far distant world—were eagerly discussing something together, with Mexone, Viona's husband, drifting rather disconsolately behind. These remaining three people brought the Cosmic Crusaders up to full strength—the most fabulous band of space rovers ever known.

"Any luck?" Viona asked, breaking off her conversation with the fair-haired, merry-eyed Thania. "Any ideas on that spaceship we're heading for?"

"We don't know anything beyond the fact that it is apparently Earthly in origin," the Amazon replied, turning back to the observation window.

"Earthly?" Thania repeated, surprised. "You mean that lovely planet *you've* come from?"

"That's correct," Abna told her. "But what it's doing

in the region of the Milky Way here is something we've yet to find out…and we'd better start slowing down," he added. "We'll be on top of it in no time."

He crossed to the switchboard and operated the necessary controls, which slowed the Ultra down in its swift advance. The others took up their stand before the mighty bowed window, gazing out onto the black infinity of space and the gray ovoid that was gradually growing bigger with every moment.

"Why not try the radio?" Mexone questioned. "That ought to show us if there's anybody aboard."

"There must be *somebody* aboard," the Amazon answered him briefly. "What we want to find out is—are they Earth people, and if so what are they doing here?"

"After all, we don't own the void," Mexone pointed out. "They have a perfect right to be here, whoever they are."

"In a ship the duplicate of ours?" The Amazon raised her eyebrows questioningly and then turned to the radio equipment. She switched it on, and then waited for a moment. Finally she drew the microphone to her.

"Attention, friend! This is the Golden Amazon of Earth speaking. Who are you? What is your purpose? Over."

The loudspeaker hummed with power and the group waited expectantly—but nothing happened. Moments passed, then in some irritation the Amazon repeated her message. Yet again there was no response.

"Strange—very strange," Abna commented. "If they are Earth people they should reply in a normal manner, using a mouth to speak with and listening with their ears… Unless we've come across a kind of *Marie Celeste* of space."

"I don't like this business at all," the Amazon said,

switching off, her face grim.

"You know something?" Viona was peering intently through the window. "That ship isn't moving at all: the surrounding stars show that. It's just drifting on cosmic currents."

"Meaning what?" the Amazon asked.

"Meaning that it doesn't seem as though there's anybody aboard that vessel to drive it. And yet," Viona went on, puzzled, "there must have been for it to have got this far."

Thania said: "We're not going to find out much carrying on in this way. Only solution is to go aboard and look for ourselves."

"True enough," the Amazon agreed, hesitating, "yet for some reason I feel reticent about doing so. I have a kind of feeling that… that it's some kind of a trap or something."

Abna, by the switchboard, grinned. "We'll be ready for it if it is. Here we go."

He turned his attention entirely to the controls and for the next half hour gave no attention to anything else. In the intervening time the others inspected the weapons in their belts and stood waiting as the Ultra, skillfully maneuvered, finally came up alongside its 'double'. Abna shifted switches—jockeying, edging, inching—until at last he had the airlock of the Ultra exactly over that of the mystery vessel. Then he threw the magnetic current into action— Immediately the doors of both machines were in absolute contact.

"Right!" Abna cut the power of the atomic motor. "We're ready to investigate."

At the Amazon's nod of assent Abna pulled over the switch that released the airlock. Slowly the ponderous mass of metal began to open inwards on its hinges until it finally clicked to a stop. Beyond was a short stretch of passage—the Ultra's conditioning chamber—and beyond that again the gray mass of the outer lock.

"Fire away," the Amazon said. "Open the outer lock, Abna."

He obeyed. The outer door opened inwards and finally clicked to a halt—but beyond there was not a vision of the void and the glittering stars but a gray metal wall.

"So far, so good," the Amazon said, moving forward. "Our job now is to find out if this mystery machine has a lock which can be opened from the outside, like the Ultra has. If so, the rest is easy. We've a clear walk-through from ship to ship."

In a matter of moments she completed the short trip down the passageway, then paused in surprise at the gray wall. Abna, right behind her, gave a slow whistle.

"So there *is* an outer lock! Exact copy of that on our Ultra."

"There's far too much exact copying for my liking," the Amazon commented. "Anyway, here goes. We'll see what happens. Have your guns ready, the rest of you," she added, glancing over her shoulder.

With that she took hold of the massive bar on the outside of the unknown spaceship's door, and forced it upwards. It finally gave a click and then became rigid. The Amazon put her shoulder to the huge door and pushed gently. As she had expected, it began to move inwards on perfectly balanced hinges.

"Just a moment," Abna said, checking her. "Suppose the air in this other ship is below pressure, or even poisoned? Once we open the second compartment door we'll get the full blast of it and we might even be overwhelmed."

"I'll be careful. Bit at a time."

Drawn on by the interest of what she was going to behold, the Amazon finally had the outer door pushed open to the limit; then she went to work on the second door, beyond the small pressure chamber in which she now stood. There was no trouble, no hiss of escaping air. Nothing mephitic came forth in the way of toxic gas—and finally the door was wide open. In silence the four looked into the control chamber beyond.

There was not a sound. There was nobody in sight. Somewhere something buzzed softly, which evidenced that power was operating, but otherwise nothing.

Finally the Amazon raised her voice and called: "Anybody here?"

No response. Abna gave a shrug as she glanced at him, and in the negative movement she found an echo of her own feelings.

"Go ahead," Viona suggested, from the rear. "Let's look the ship over."

Again a presentiment crossed the Amazon's mind, but she ignored it as imagination born of the unusual circumstances. Gripping her protonic gun tightly, the others following behind her, she padded across to the narrow passage beyond the control room. Here, as in the Ultra, were the storerooms and bedrooms.

And so it went on—to the observatory in the top of the ship, to the power room where the fuses and 'innards' of the vessel were located. In almost every respect the machine was a duplicate of the Ultra—

Then suddenly something happened! Just as the Amazon was leading the way back into the control room, intent on examining the power plant. It was as she crossed from the passage to the control room, the others still behind her, there was a sudden crescendo in the faint humming which was constantly noticeable.

After that, things began to happen at an incredible speed. There came two distinct and heavy thumps as both inner and outer doors suddenly slammed shut. Hardly had this happened, hardly indeed had the quintet decided that something usual was happening, when the mystery ship suddenly started moving. Nor was it a slow and orderly process, but a hurtling forward to ever increasing velocity.

Unable to help themselves, the five sprawled on the floor at the edge of the control room, trying giddily to understand what had happened. Aided by their vast strength, the Amazon and Abna both tried to reach the switchboard, and though they managed a few dragging feet of distance to the center of the control room the appalling velocity of the machine proved too much for them. They were crushed down with the feeling that thousands of tons were on their backs. They flattened on the floor and seemed as though their very ribs would be driven into the metal.

Until finally outraged lungs and hearts could stand no more. The quintet blacked out completely and, with that, the involuntary muscles took over and allowed the merest scrap of air to filter into their lungs. Hearts beat too—but slowly.

And meanwhile, without as yet an explanation for its amazing behavior, the space machine flashed through the gulfs of space at a speed beyond imagining, approaching that of light itself, a momentum so inconceivable that even the gigantic mass of the Milky Way seemed to recede into the distance.

The Amazon had time for one last agonized thought, as she and the other Crusaders slipped into unconsciousness. Acceleration to near light speed suggested that the ship was building up speed to enable it to plunge into hyperspace. And so it proved.

Then, and only then, as acceleration gave place to constant speed, did the five begin to revive. The terrible weight lifted from lungs and hearts and the Crusaders dazedly opened their eyes.

The Amazon was the first to completely recover. Muscles and reason reintegrated themselves and she struggled to her feet. She was conscious of passing surprise that she was not weightless as she had expected. Instead gravity was Earth normal, so presumably the ship was fitted with nullifiers, in the same fashion as the Ultra.

Puzzled, allowing the others to recover in their own way, she went across to the observation window and peered out, the slanted unbreakable glass preventing any reflection from the control room within. She smiled to herself at the vision of what registered on her eyes as swirling gray mist, but which was the enigmatic nothingness of hyperspace. Her suspicion had been confirmed. They were flying through hyperspace at an inconceivable velocity in relation to the normal universe.

But what was their destination?

"Well?" asked Abna's voice beside her. "Where are we—and even more interesting, how did we get here?"

"At the moment I've not the least idea, but since we're in hyperspace we must be traveling faster than light."

"Some lick!" Abna agreed; then he frowned. "But why? What caused all this? And if we've entered hyperspace we must have left our own Ultra behind." He met the Amazon's eyes. "Do you suppose it was a trap?"

"Of course it was!" She clenched her fist on the window ledge. "I had a presentiment that there was something wrong, but instead of heeding it I went straight on—and this is the result. I'm furious with myself for having walked into this with my eyes wide open. What about the power plant? Any chance of stopping it?"

She moved actively across to it and Abna followed. There then began for them a series of alarming discoveries—during which time Viona, Mexone and Thania recovered sufficiently to help them in their investigations.

The first shock lay in the discovery that the power plant could not be interfered with. It was obviously consuming copper blocks, the same as the Ultra's plant, but unlike the Ultra the whole power unit was covered with an unbreakable transparent cover against which even proton guns were useless.

The same transparent protection was over the switchboard, again preventing any attempt at interference.

"A very clever idea," the Amazon commented bitterly. "The only way to get through this cover—and the one over the power plant—is to use instruments like those on the Ultra, and since the Ultra is no longer with us there's nothing we can do. We just have to leave it dead alone."

"Leave things alone!" Viona echoed. "But we can't! We've no idea what we may run into to."

"We can't run into anything whilst we're in hyperspace anyway," the Amazon commented. "Presumably we'll drop back into normal space when we've covered sufficient distance and reach a pre-determined point—one that our abductors must have planned. The only thing we can do is to go with it, and keep our fingers crossed."

"How do you suppose things happen like they do?" Mexone asked, rubbing his head in bewilderment. "I mean, the way the ship suddenly started moving, the fact that it stays on course, the fact that the airlock shut, and so on. Something must have caused those things to happen."

The Amazon glanced about her then finally nodded

rather grimly towards complicated electronic equipment, covered like every other important unit with a protective transparency.

"There, I imagine, is the answer," she said, crossing over to it; then as she studied its glittering complexity she added, "No doubt of it. This thing here is an electronic brain of very high order. The heart of this vessel, in fact."

Abna was peering closely at the panel; then after a while he gave a low whistle. The Amazon looked at him in surprise.

"What is it?" she inquired.

"Something very interesting. I was just looking at this almost microscopic manufacturer's name on the panel—it reads 'Sawley Limited, Electronic Engineers, London'."

The Amazon gave a start, then looked for herself. In a moment the others had done likewise—then finally it was Viona who voiced all their thoughts.

"Then—then this spaceship has come unmanned, from Earth!"

"Exactly," the Amazon agreed. "And unless I'm very much mistaken it will return to Earth on the same course— a course calculated with computers without a vestige of error."

Silence—and complete bewilderment. A ship from Earth finding its way to the First Galaxy without an accident, unmanned? It was impossible.

"No, it isn't impossible," the Amazon said presently, as she followed this line of thought. "Untold centuries have passed by on Earth since we left, even though the capital of Britain is still obviously called London. The science on Earth must by now be of immense scope, hence this vessel... Don't forget that in our varied experiences we have traveled thousands of years in Time, apart from the Timefactors involved in space travel, and there are many. Yes, many centuries have gone by since we left Earth."

"After all," Viona mused, "if a guided missile could hit a target thousands of miles away back in the twenty-first century, why shouldn't a spaceship reach us in the Milky Way considering the progress which must have been made?"

Mexone said: "Yes, but why was it done? That's what mystifies me."

"Suppose," Abna suggested, "we try and reason this business out. It is quite clear that we came aboard this ship out of sheer curiosity. Somebody—presumably the ones who sent this ship—counted on us doing just that. The moment we did it, photo-electric cells took care of the rest. The airlock shut and the power plant suddenly assumed full power. Presumably, this same automatic system cast the Ultra away from its magnetic attachment to this ship, and probably repulsed it to a certain distance, beyond the limits where it could be chained by this vessel's mass and be caught up in the field generated by our hyper-drive engines. After that, after we lost consciousness, this vessel must have approached the speed of light—and then automatically plunged into hyperspace."

"And now we're nailed here waiting for the next," the Amazon snapped. "It's not a happy thought—and for once in our lives we're powerless to do anything about it."

Abna did not seem to hear her. He slowly posed a question:

"The problem now is: Who can it be on Earth that so suddenly wants us?"

The Amazon moved impatiently to the window and stared out on to the swirling enigma of non-space. She still spoke with the pent-up anger she was undoubtedly feeling.

"Whatever it is, there could have been a better way than this!" she declared. "Why steal our vessel and everything we possess? It amounts to—interstellar kidnapping!"

Viona said: "Perhaps there wasn't any other way of getting at us? At our colossal distance how could we be contacted? A guided interstellar missile would be the only answer to that one."

The Amazon did not reply. She was too angry—not only with the situation but with herself as well. The fact that she had walked right into the trap was not a pleasant realization for her.

"Anyway," Thania said, in the heavy silence, "since we seem to be heading for Earth there's one person who won't grumble—and that's me. I've always wanted to see your home planet, Amazon. From what you've told me it must be very beautiful."

"I'm interested, too," Mexone reflected.

"It was beautiful once—when we left it," Abna said, thinking. "How it will be now I can't say. Changed beyond recognition, I suppose."

The Amazon gave a grim glance, then she came over to where Abna was standing. There was something in her manner that compelled the others' attention.

"I think it's about time all of you stopped looking at this business through rose-tinted spectacles! Whoever wants us has stopped at nothing to get us, and sacrificed our ship to do it. That alone does not suggest that we're going to find friends waiting for us on Earth. I'm prepared for trouble—lots of it!"

"Aren't you always?" Abna asked, with a good-humored smile. "Not that I blame you, but whatever the trouble may be—if any—we'll deal with it."

"How? With no weapons worth speaking of!"

"One thing seems pretty clear," Viona remarked, studying the power plant through its transparent covering. "Whoever sent this ship knows a great deal about the Ultra. It's pretty nearly an exact duplicate."

"Pretty nearly, but not altogether," Abna responded. "It's a copy of the Ultra as it was when we left Earth, but during our travels we have added many instruments which are not duplicated here—the Zero-Thought Amplifier for one. Another thing is that we had to accelerate to near light speed before entering hyperspace. In our latest Ultra we can enter hyperspace at will—although, of course, the faster we are traveling in normal space at the point of entry, the faster we travel in hyperspace. That doesn't signify particularly at the moment—though it does indicate we may be embarked on a very long journey across space."

At this the Amazon, who had been gazing moodily through the window, suddenly gave a start.

"That's a disturbing thought," she commented. "That awful weapon, the Zero-Thought Amplifier, is there on the Ultra for any space wanderer to use it he wishes, and we can't do a thing about it."

"No," Abna agreed. "We can't—at the moment. We may think of something later. Meantime, there's no sense in worrying over something we cannot alter."

The Amazon had not Abna's calm philosophy. She did worry, quite a lot, even though she hid her feelings. The thought of the immensely valuable and potentially dangerous Ultra being somewhere behind in the void, for any space-rover to take over, was disquieting in the extreme.

"I wonder," Thania said, "if our abductor friends have provided for our comfort during the journey? It's about time we found some food… Coming, Viona?"

"Sure thing!"

In another moment both young women had departed on their second—and much more intensive—tour of the vessel. Mexone watched them go, then he wandered over to Abna and the Amazon by the window.

"Well, how bad is it really?" he inquired. "Is there anything you haven't said because they were there?"

"Nothing at all," the Amazon answered. "They're as capable as the rest of us at hearing the facts. We've been in too many tight corners for them not to know the truth."

Mexone gazed through the window at the interminable writhing gray mist. At last he asked a question.

"How long at this rate before we reach Earth?"

"It would need computers to work that out," the Amazon replied. "There are none here that are accessible to us. From what I remember of our original position in space, it could be several weeks, or even months before the Earth-system is reached. That's assuming that is our destination, of course. In the meantime let's hope there's food somewhere on board or we'll be dead before we arrive…"

She had hardly finished speaking before Viona and Thania re-appeared in the control room doorway, their arms piled up with sealed boxes. One, however, was open and Thania was sampling the contents avidly.

"Food in plenty," she announced, seeing the Amazon's look. "Whoever planned this trip has seen we're provided for—and there's also a big stock of bottles containing some kind of drink." She dumped her boxes alongside Viona's on the control room table. "I'll go back and get them."

She hurried out again and Abna raised an eyebrow at the Amazon. She sighed and then gave a shrug.

"Evidently we're to be alive after all," she commented. "We'd better sample this food—which ought to be edible enough if it's from Earth. Then after that we'll settle back and see what happens next."

CHAPTER 2

Return to Earth

So for the Crusaders there began a wearisome period of waiting and watching—of sleeping and eating, whilst waiting for the ship to drop out of hyperspace. It happened, however, that the Amazon was very much wrong in her calculations, since it was nearly three months before the swirling gray mist of hyperspace was replaced—after a brief, painful jolt—with the star-flecked black of normal space. Immediately the space machine began to fire its reactors, slowing up in its hurtling onrush. And that could surely mean only one thing—the Earth system must be approaching. This time the Crusaders were able to take to the bunks, to more comfortably withstand the deceleration.

The Amazon was the first to spot the yellowish G-type dwarf sun that was the Earth's primary, and the planets themselves scattered at varying distances from it. And still the space ship flashed onward but at greatly reduced speed.

"I might be wrong," Abna said critically, surveying the solar system ahead, "but I get the impression that we're off course! I've been watching Earth for some time now and it's slowly veering off to the left. It doesn't look like Earth is our destination after all."

The Amazon studied the view for a moment or two,

Mexone, Viona and Thania grouped about her. Finally she nodded.

"Yes, I think you're right," she agreed; then her face became troubled. "But if we are not heading for Earth then where *are* we bound for?"

"Sounds ridiculous," Abna said, "but I'd say Mercury is our destination. Notice it there?" He shaded the sun from his eyes to take in the eccentric little planet so close to the flaming orb of day. "By the time we've covered a few more million miles—on our present course—Mercury will have swung inwards to be dead in line with us."

"But—but Mercury is a hell planet!" Viona protested. "It rotates so slowly that it's alternately frozen on its dark side and scorched on the other. And a dead world; we know that from past experience. Surely there'd be no purpose in sending us to a graveyard like that?"

"No purpose at all," the Amazon agreed, her face still troubled. "However, there does exist the possibility that whoever charted our course through space made a mistake, with the result that we are going to by-pass Earth and, as Abna has said, probably land on Mercury instead."

"Land on it!" Mexone echoed. "You mean crash into it, at a speed like this!"

"As to that, we can only hope that we slow down. If we don't, then I'm afraid we're finished for there's nothing we can do to control this vessel—and smashing the protective coverings and fiddling with the controls may only serve to make death more certain."

"I've been thinking about why we've veered off course," Abna said, "And I think there may be an explanation. Mercury is a very dense, rocky planet, with a metallic core like the Earth. It's quite different from most of the other planets in our system in that it also possesses a full-blown magnetic field. If our ship's computers were set to react to a magnetic field, they could have mistaken Mercury's for the Earth!"

The tenseness of the situation was not long in communicating itself to each member of the little band—but none passed any comment. Used to the threat of death in various forms they were each coldly philosophical, weighing up the chances with a scientific detachment. And none too good the chances looked as time went on.

They none of them deserted the window, except for hasty meals. Their whole concentration was on the system ahead of them and the fact that there was no further decrease in speed. At roughly half the speed of light they flashed past the orbits of Pluto and Neptine, then progressively past the orbits of the other giant outer worlds in turn.

So past the orbit of ruddy Mars, after which there was a noticeable clicking from the power plant and a corresponding decrease in speed. The Amazon glanced up sharply.

"That seems to suggest that Earth—the next planet in line—is actually our intended stopping place," she said, "but we're still off course by several millions of miles."

She was right—and by the time another series of meals and brief rests had come and gone the fact was more than obvious. Earth was sinking away into space and the automatically driven spaceship was moving on at a greatly reduced speed towards the orbit of Venus—and beyond that, hardly visible against the glare of the unmasked sun with its mighty twirling prominences, was little Mercury. Right in line—the apparent terminus.

"Well, what do we do?" Abna asked quietly, when all of them had assembled at the window to assess the situation. "Just sit and take what's coming to us or smash these switchboards in an effort to get control?"

"We'd better grin and bear it," the Amazon decided, after a moment. "We said before that smashing these switchboards may only make matters worse…" She studied the tiny little planet with her eyes narrowed against the unholy light of the sun; then she added, "On the off chance we land all in one piece we'd better look around for what spacesuits there are. Conditions on that airless little world will be far from pleasant if the vessel is no longer airtight."

They all turned actively, the threat of very-near Mercury weighing heavily on their minds, and began a search of the ship. Certainly they did not expect to find spacesuits since, if the trip had ended at Earth, as presumably was the intention, they would not need spacesuits anyway. Yet, to their amazement, they finally located a dozen of them in one of the many lockers near the sleeping quarters. The Amazon began to drag them forth one by one and handed them over, her mind casting round for explanation as to the reason for the miracle.

"Only one explanation," she said finally. "These must have been put here in case, for some reason, we had to examine the outside of the vessel. There might have been damage from meteoroids, for instance, or some such trouble as that."

The others nodded, not particularly concerned with reasons. Their own realization was that if the ship landed without smashing them completely in the process they still had a chance to survive, even if some of the vessel's plates should be buckled enough to allow precious air to escape.

The moment they had the spacesuits on and the helmet radios linked up they tramped back to the control room to survey the picture, and were startled to behold Mercury filling all of the space in front of them—a rocky, arid little planet, the face turned to the baleful sun scorching hot, and the other dark side plunged into freezing darkness.

"We're still slowing down," Abna said, with a glance at the instruments through their protective covering.

The Amazon glanced at him through her transparent helmet faceplate. "Just as well that we are. Even as it is, we'll still know all about it when we hit those rocks."

The others nodded grimly and looked at each other, none of them really afraid, but definitely tensed up and ready for the unexpected. Finally, they all followed the Amazon's example as she snapped a switch on her helmet and caused a purple shield to drop in position over her face. This made things easier and prevented damage to the eyes from the appalling nearness of the raging sun.

"We've one thing to be grateful for," Abna remarked, after a while. "If our course had been a few more degrees to the cosmic east we'd have passed Mercury by too wide a margin for his mass to have pulled us. That would have meant flying straight into the sun, and nothing could have saved us."

His observation was only too true and it had a sobering effect on the others. They even felt more cheerful, realizing what they had escaped... Then depression clamped down again as Mercury swept ever nearer, and nearer, until they could see the planet as a huge ball bisected by light and dark. On the one side the almost totally airless night, and on the other gigantic seams and gorges split here and there where natural metals, even including tough tungsten, boiled under the relentless glare of sun. So it had always been for untold centuries. Mercury was a planet in name only—lifeless, dehydrated, sucked dry by the flaming giant which forever ruled only a scant 33 million miles distant.

The final stages of the space machine's journey were swift and terrifying. There was no rush and whine of cleavage through the atmosphere, for of course there was none. There was only a vision of twirling landscape, crazy shadows, bottomless ravines—and then a concussion of cataclysmic violence. Plates and seams creaked under the onslaught and the Crusaders, although strapped in their bunks and with their pressurized suits to protect them, were violently shaken up—though they did not sustain anything worse than bruises, and most certainly they did not lose consciousness.

For the rest there was a complete silence. The power plant had ceased to operate. Through the giant window sunlight streamed in a flood of intolerable effulgence, intolerable even through the purple helmet-shields.

"So far, so good," came the Amazon's muttered voice in the audiophone as she struggled to her feet. "From the First Galaxy to Mercury in one hop…"

The others struggled up around her, watching as her bloated, space-suited figure went over to the window. At the exterior thermometer reading she stopped and there was a whistle of amazement in her audiophone.

"Five hundred and forty degrees, and still rising!" she gasped. "Thank heaven for these insulated spacesuits or we'd perish like flies on a griddle!"

She turned away from the thermometer and finally gained the window. Here, for a moment, she stood surveying. The vessel had fallen in the midst of a ridged plateau ranged on the curiously-near horizon by tall, friendless hills. Their peaks reared like the teeth of a saw against the totally black and star-smothered sky. Gleaming amongst the stars somewhat dimly was a noticeable green one, which was undoubtedly Earth itself.

As for the rest it was a molten wilderness. The very ground was boiling—a seething magma like the inside of a volcano. All the various minerals of the planet were in complete flux, sizzling under the merciless rays of a sun only 33 million miles distant.

"In fact, the perfect hell-planet," Abna said, coming to Amazon's side and gazing through his purple face-shield. "A charming spot on which to land with no weapons or means of moving."

The Amazon was about to answer when Viona interrupted her with an urgent exclamation. She was standing towards the rear of the control room, gazing down the passage, which led to the sleeping quarters.

"Something's cracked somewhere!" she exclaimed in alarm. "Take a look!"

In a moment the others were with her, gazing in grim silence at a fracture in the spaceship's floor, through which molten metal and deposits were forcing themselves relentlessly. And as the furiously hot quagmire oozed through, the metal of the ship itself dissolved like lead before a blowtorch.

"We've done more damage than we thought," Abna said at last, looking about him. "The furnace state of the ground on the sunward side of the planet is melting the ship like wax. Yes! It goes on right to the end of the corridor there! See? The whole back of the ship is involved."

The Amazon glanced behind her into the control room. "Yet not the front part, from the look of it. Control room's safe—so far. Now you come to look at it the floor tilts slightly backwards. That means the rear end is sunk in this stuff but not the front, which is evidently clear of the ground."

Viona said quickly: "We're sinking anyway—and pretty rapidly. Once we land in this stuff we're done for. Our spacesuits will go whoof and that will be the end of everything…"

For a moment or two the five watched the bubbling mass creeping ever so slowly towards them; then the Amazon looked about her in sudden urgency. Finally she said:

"There's only one solution, and we've got to act fast to save ourselves. We've got to get control of this power plant and get into space whilst we're still safe! The ship won't be airtight any more but since we're in spacesuits that won't matter. We didn't dare smash these protective coverings before for fear of what would happen—but now it's imperative before we go down in this molten bog." She wheeled suddenly back into the control room. "Quick, all of you! Get busy! Try using the proton-guns first."

She whipped her own proton gun from her belt and went to work on the transparent covering shielding the power plant. At the same time the others directed their energies to the control board, but even so it was a matter of several minutes of continuous blasting from the proton guns before their tremendous destructive energy had an effect. And even then it was limited. A slight area of the covering began to crumble, leaving practically ninety percent of the rest of the covering still intact.

"This is too slow for comfort," the Amazon decided presently, slipping her weapon back in her belt and glancing towards the deadly tide of gray metal still spreading inwards. "Now we've got a hand-hold maybe our strength can tear the covering out of its fixtures."

Even as she was speaking she had hold of the substance and, bracing her heavily booted feet against the base of the power plant she threw all her vast strength into an effort to tear the covering free. Seconds and then minutes passed as she wrestled and strained, with only short pauses in between for renewal of strength.

The others did not help her: They were too busy dealing with the covering over the switchboard—pulling and tugging at the stuff with their hands locked in the small area they had managed to blast away. So, for a long time, the battle went on—superhuman strength against the enormously tough transparent material. Gloved hands pulled with enormous power; muscles cracked under the effort—but finally enough of the substance had been pulled away to allow room for maneuver. As far as the Amazon was concerned, immediately this happened, she opened the matrix of the power plant and took the spare copper block from the emergency clamps just inside the plant itself. In an instant she had placed it in the matrix's jaws and closed them.

"Power enough and to spare," she explained, as the others glanced in her direction. "And we'll need it. There'll be a lot of drag from this morass we've dropped in… How about you? How are you going on?"

"We can reach the switches, anyhow," Abna responded. "The job now will be to understand them."

"That may not be so difficult." The Amazon crossed to his side. "Since this vessel is almost identical in design to the first Ultra the system of control will probably be similar. It seems quite obvious that the Ultra has inspired the planning."

"Once it's freed from automatic control," Viona said, busy on the job of tracing the automatic control conduits. "The connection seems to be to the power plant itself, and it went out of action the moment we hit Mercury. I'll have this lot clear in a moment."

"There was probably some exterior device which broke the contact when we landed." The Amazon was busy studying the switchboard. "I'm quite convinced that the whole project was intended to land us on Earth, but it badly misfired."

Mexone, who had moved to the control room door to survey the back corridor, suddenly gave a cry of consternation.

"We're going to get cremated if we don't hurry!" he cried. "This lava stuff has flooded nearly all the back of the ship and it's still coming!"

The Amazon glanced at him, suffered an obvious moment of indecision, then seemed to make up her mind.

"We'll risk it," she said, and glanced at Viona. "Got those connections freed yet?"

"Yes—we're okay in that department."

The Amazon promptly reached behind the torn protective covering of the switchboard with her enormously gloved hand and snapped three switches. Then she pulled what was clearly a power lever. At the same moment Viona tore away the last traces of a mass of wires that seemed as though they made contact with automatic transmission gadgets.

The five waited, then their eyes brightened as the power plant came into whining life. The Amazon watched through her purple face-shield and then snapped another switch. With this action the power plant increased its whine to a roar and the entire vessel trembled violently.

For a moment there was a sensation of it straining enormously, then suddenly it was free—but only as half a ship! The other half still lay in the molten morass in which it had fallen. The five, unwarned by any sound in the airless vacuum had no knowledge of the ship's 'broken back' until they found themselves gazing into the enormous void a foot or two away from them. Instantly they clutched at wall supports. They were in the nose of the machine, and that was all. Everything else had gone, left behind on the mad sun-and-frost-cracked planet from which they were whirling.

"Well we got away anyhow," Abna said, going cautiously to the opening and inspecting the damage. "The rocket jets have snapped as well, but they seem to be firing all right. "I suppose," he added reflectively, "this must be the first time we've ever traveled in half a ship with the end open to space!"

The others did not answer for the moment; they were too surprised to think straight. Then the Amazon turned once more and groped around the switchboard. Abruptly, under her ministrations, the vessel dived away in a leftward arc.

"Sorry," she apologized, straightening the ship up again. "I was just making a test. The controls answer perfectly, so even if the jets are severed we're still able to steer."

Thania moved carefully to the open end of the ship, clutching projections as she went. Finally she reached the point where she could see out into the void. She surveyed the wondrous emptiness with its multimillions of stars and flaring sun. There was awe in her eyes behind the purple shield.

"Don't worry—you can't fall out," Viona said dryly walking to her side without holding on to supports, "The nullifiers, what's left of 'em, are still working under the control room floor so as to keep gravity at about normal. As for space, you simply can't fall into it. The mass of the ship has a hold on you."

Thania said: "It's all very wonderful, yet somehow scarifying, if you know what I mean. I wanted adventure, and I'm certainly getting it!"

"In chunks," Viona agreed; then she turned and looked

at her mother. "Where are you going to head for, mother? Earth?"

"That's my intention," the Amazon nodded; then her face became grimmer behind the purple shield. "Then maybe we'll find out the reason for the theft of the Ultra and our own inconvenience…" She looked at the dials measuring the velocity and then added, "My guess is that this old hulk we're traveling in will reach Earth in about 16 hours—and then, Thania, you can gratify your wish to see the world from which Viona and I came, and Abna is descended from. But I don't think it will be anything like the world we once knew."

"Whether it is or not," Abna said, "it will at least be a planet we understand, and that will be something—for a change!"

* * * *

For many hours the fantastic little wreck of a spaceship held to its course, a fact only made possible by all the instruments and power plant being centralized in the front half of the ship—whilst storerooms and dormitories had been in the section that had snapped away.

And, mostly in silence, devoid now of their purple masks, the five space-suited Crusaders watched the massive globe of Earth grow ever larger until after a while they were able to distinguish known continents and oceans, clouds floating across them at intervals.

"From here," Abna said, brooding over the scene like some weird, space-suited god, "there doesn't appear to be much change—not as far as the topography is concerned, anyway."

The Amazon said: "Only a cataclysm would be likely to change continents and oceans. The actual changes, I imagine, will be in civilization itself. And that we can't view without a telescope. Have to wait until we get there."

"Where do you think will be a good place to land?" Viona asked after a moment, and the Amazon surveyed. Finally she answered:

"I should think London—or near it—would be best. That's where we've always operated from, and it was from there that we departed."

With this in mind she turned presently to the control board and eased her hand under the covering. She flicked various switches more or less experimentally and so gradually changed the 'Hulk's' course until at last it was drifting over the British Isles and descending slowly from a height of about 150 miles. Gradually, too, as the descent continued, the sun became a normal golden ball and the weirdness of the prominences and incredible grandeur of the zodiacal light disappeared. In a word, atmosphere was once more present.

"In spite of everything, in spite of this fantastic object that's carrying us—that scene below still looks like home," the Amazon murmured through her audiophone.

"Yet, I'm afraid, a home without those we once knew," Abna sighed. "Chris Wilson and his wife Beatrice, their daughter Ethel and Barry Schofield, Commander and Ruth Kerrigan—all those who made the first Dodd Space-line possible, must have all gone by now."

"1t makes you wonder if virtual immortality is such a boon after all," the Amazon sighed, and became silent for a moment as memories of the very early days came crowding nostalgically into her mind.

"Know something?" Viona remarked presently. "It's night down in England. Now the atmosphere's present you can see where the darkness ends."

"Perhaps be to our advantage," the Amazon said, her eyes on the huge crescent of dark, which signified where the sun had not yet risen. Astronomically speaking, Earth was at the stage where the old Earth lay in the new Earth's arms.

So the machine descended, mile by mile, then by the thousands of feet, coming presently into the soft swathing darkness of the lower atmosphere and out of the glare of the sun. Down and ever down, the winking lights of England far below and the gray, gleaming sea on every side of the island. Here and there aircraft, and perhaps even spacecraft, floated like fireflies and were gone, having no suspicion of the weird craft and the five Crusaders so close to them.

The hulk did not land near London. It struck the sea to the southeast of England and north of the English Channel. The Amazon was entirely to blame for the mistake, yet it was purely the outcome of trying to handle a vessel that did not answer too well to the controls… The finish of the journey came with a tremendous thwack of water and instantly the hulk plunged under, forcing the five into the depths. Two things saved them from drowning—the buoyant protection of their spacesuits and the hulk's open end.

Like corks they bobbed to the surface of the water, and once again the tremendous buoyancy of their spacesuits made swimming a simple matter. In fact it was not so much swimming as traction. By the movement of their bloated arms and legs they made steady progress towards the looming grayness in the distance that was the shore.

Impelled by such superhuman muscles the swim did not take long. Ten minutes later the five were scrambling up a sloping shingle in the shadow of gigantic cliffs.

"Better get rid of these suits," the Amazon said, and set

the example by removing her own. When she was finally free of it and standing in her black space-tights she took the suit and threw it in the water nearby. It began to sink and was swiftly carried away by the Channel current.

"Well," Abna said finally, when the rest of the space-suits had been thrown away, "we're back on Earth. And as far as you are concerned, Thania, we welcome you to it."

"It's very much like my own world," the teenager murmured, looking about her in the gloom. "Warm and comfortable—and there is a sense of freedom."

The Amazon said: "The sense of freedom may be an illusion. This lonely Sussex coast where we've landed is no guide at all." She surveyed for a moment and then added, "From the feel of the air it is evidently summer, and that means the darkness will be of only short duration. We'd better strike inland and see what we can find—above all the explanation for us being in this extraordinary situation."

"We've neither food nor drink with us," Mexone reminded, and at that the Amazon laughed a little.

"That's hardly a problem when you're on your own world, and know exactly what is poisonous and what's not. We'll find something, never fear... Let's start moving, shall we?"

She led the way through the shingle to the cliffs nearby, looming against the misty stars. After a moment or two she found an acclivity and began ascending it, the others behind her. Compared to the climbing difficulties with which they had had to contend sometimes on other worlds, this steep ascent up an English cliff was only a trifle, and in a matter of ten minutes they had gained the flat grassland at the summit.

Without speaking, they looked about them, the soft

summer night wind blowing on their faces. Somehow, in a manner which none of them could pinpoint, they had a feeling of strangeness, of having come to an Earth which was totally devoid of familiarity.

"What's that over there?" Abna asked, pointing. "Looks like some kind of Coliseum with a town behind."

The others looked in the way he indicated, straining their eyes in the darkness—all except the Amazon. Her gift for seeing in the dark made the distant scene fairly clear.

About two or three miles away across the down-land there seemed to be the edge of a town. There was first, as Abna had pointed out, a mighty structure that looked remarkably like the Coliseum of Rome, and behind it, terrace upon terrace, were buildings reaching into the distance. Some had lights; some were dark. Certainly they were unlike anything known in England—as it had once been.

"Better go closer and find out—" Viona started to say; then she stopped abruptly and glanced above her. The others did likewise, intently watching a huge, silent aircraft as it swept out of the darkness and headed for the strange city in the distance. It dropped out of sight just beyond the Coliseum-like building, the signal lights gleaming clearly on its stubbed, set-back wings.

"Things seem to be reasonably civilized, anyway," the Amazon murmured. "There wouldn't be aircraft if that were not so. Let's look further."

They began to advance swiftly, prepared for any kind of trouble there might be, and in a matter of fifteen minutes, moving at a jog-trot, they reached the outer wall of the 'Coliseum' and stood surveying it—a mighty wall of stone now they could observe it clearly, towering perhaps 100 feet into the air.

CHAPTER 3

Battle of the Tigers

"No getting over that," the Amazon said. "Except by aircraft, that is. I just wonder what they're afraid of."

"There may be a door somewhere," Mexone suggested. "Suppose we take a look?"

They started to prowl round the base of the wall, meantime asking themselves many questions and failing to answer any of them. Whence had come this strange mixture of Romanesque architecture and super-modern airplanes? The two things just didn't jell, any more than did this fantastic wall, mighty enough to keep out a mastodon.

Dawn was just commencing to streak the eastern sky when Mexone gave a sudden exclamation. He stopped and pointed.

"Look—a ladder! Down the wall."

He was right. In another moment the five had reached it—a metal ladder staked into the wall and reaching to its top.

"Here goes," the Amazon said, with a glance at the lightening sky. "At least we'll get a view of what's going on beyond the wall, anyway—and we might even discover a few explanations for ourselves."

She started to climb swiftly, immediately followed by

Abna and then the younger ones. Once the summit of the wall was reached—and it was at least three feet thick—they stood gazing, impressed again by the amazing resemblance to Rome of old.

In the immediate foreground, practically beneath them on the other side of the wall, was a vast amphitheatre, the wall entirely surrounding it. Stretching away from this amphitheatre were rows upon rows of empty stone seats, and at the far side of the 'Coliseum' there straddled a gigantic and hideous idol, arms aloft and legs astride—the legs indeed forming the sides of a high doorway of metal bars. And beyond again, in the brightening light, were terraces of buildings. And again beyond this were the evidences of a seemingly civilized city with all the modern paraphernalia of streets, traffic ways, and—atop the taller buildings—beacon towers and radar direction-finders.

"At a guess," the Amazon said finally, "I'd say a curious mixture of ancient and modern, though how such a thing comes to be I can't imagine. This place down here is an exact replica of the Coliseum amphitheatre of Rome… Say," she finished, staring intently into the distance, "isn't that the 'plane we saw come down?"

The others saw after a moment what she meant. Something with wings spread was just beyond the gateway between the feet of the idol. And that something was in a big, square area that could have been a landing field.

"Plane it is," Abna confirmed; then he raised an eyebrow at the Amazon. "Are you thinking what I'm thinking?"

"Why not? If we could get our hands on that 'plane and do a bit of exploring we could find out what kind of a setup there is on Earth these days—and it would be a much quicker way of getting to London, too. Come on—what are we waiting for?"

She started to move along the wall but Abna grabbed her back. She gave him a questioning look.

Abna said: "No telling who might be watching us up here. We're just clay pigeons on top of this wall now the daylight's coming—and we're not dressed like city dwellers either. We'd stand a much better chance of reaching that 'plane by crossing the amphitheater below."

The Amazon reflected and then nodded briefly at the wisdom of the idea.

"Right enough," she said finally. "I'll lead the way."

With that she turned to where the ladder continued down the other side of the wall and began to descend swiftly with the others just above her. The moment they were all on the amphitheater floor they could not help but remark to themselves how completely like the center of the great Coliseum of Nero's time the place was, with the endless empty seats facing down upon them.

"I'd very much like to know what goes on here," the Amazon remarked. "However, there's no time now. The daylight's increasing with every moment."

She started forward again at a swift, lithe run—then as she and the others reached the approximate center of the arena they slid to a standstill, glancing about them sharply as a voice—English, of course—boomed at them from a concealed loudspeaker. Concealed also was the speaker, who evidently had been watching.

"Interlopers are neither desired nor encouraged!" the voice shouted. "Prepare to do battle!"

"Battle?" the Amazon repeated, frowning. "With whom?"

"Perhaps we—" Thania started to say; then her voice broke off in a frightened gasp as she caught sight of something. "Look over there!"

The Amazon glanced towards a side gateway, heavily barred, some distance away. It had been half raised and the Amazon felt for her proton gun as she watched three slinking tigers coming into view. Then there were four—and finally half a dozen. Magnificent brutes all of them, their muzzles twitching as they finally beheld the five Crusaders. For a second or two cold human eyes stared into green ferocious orbs.

"Evidently tigers haven't vanished from Earth," Abna murmured, never shifting his gaze from them.

"What—what do we do?" Thania questioned, her voice clearly shaken as she gripped her proton-gun tenaciously.

"We keep going straight on, my dear. Once we turn tail we're done. I rather think we can master these brutes by the power of mind alone," Abna said. "Agreed, Vi?"

"Agreed." Her voice was taut, matter-of-fact. She started to walk forward again, taking care to keep her gun at the ready. Thania slid to a position behind Abna's vast figure. So far she had not experienced at first hand the power of mind over deadly animals... Certainly it would be the quieter way. Once the guns were used the animals would shake the echoes with their death-cries.

There was little doubt that the whole performance was being watched—possibly with amazement—by the one who had spoken over the loudspeaker. If so, he was certainly getting his money's worth as steadily, calmly, the five advanced until the snarling cats were directly in their path.

"Stop!" Abna ordered suddenly. "Stare the brutes out so we can get beyond them. Don't relax for a second!"

So it began, the silent battle between man and beast. The seconds passed on but the tigers did not flinch. They snarled, they grumbled in their throats, but they did not attempt to spring. In fact there was little doubt that had things gone on as they were the beasts would finally have cowered back whence they came—defeated by the cold high intelligence of those they sought to destroy.

But something happened—and it was the teenage Thania who was the cause of it. She had not, as yet, the unwavering staying power of her comrades, even though science had given her the same strength of body. Abruptly she broke down and with that a scream of terror escaped her. Instantly the tension was broken—and the beasts sprang!

The Amazon went down on her back with a crash, the proton gun flying out of her hand. As she fell she had the presence of mind from long experience to double up her legs, which she thrust outwards again with all her force as one of the tigers charged upon her. Instantly it was flung backwards, half winded by the terrific blow in the stomach it received.

Out of the corner of her eye the Amazon glimpsed Abna, Viona, Mexone, and even Thania all struggling for their lives against the clawing fury about them—then she had to force herself to deal with the savage brute who seemed to have selected her as a target. She scrambled to one knee, decided her proton gun was too far away for her to be able to reach it and prepared to meet the tiger's second spring full on. She waited until the last moment and then flung herself to one side. The tiger landed with claws outspread and jowls slavering, obviously mystified that the prey was not there.

A second or two afterwards he found the prey—on his back. The Amazon jumped astride him, locked her feet under his powerful body and her forearms round his neck. Then she strained with every vestige of her terrible strength.

Within moments the tiger must have realized that in this golden-hued human with the soft flesh he had somebody as strong as himself to deal with. He began to wriggle, snarling venomously, as the Amazon pulled tighter and tighter with her forearms. The glossy, muscular back of the tiger began to bend from the fleck downwards until finally there was a sharp crack and a final scream of death as the brute relaxed in the dust.

The Amazon stood up, brushed the streaming perspiration from her face, then dived for her proton gun. Grasping it in her hand, cold fury on her face, she fired at the remaining beasts as they tried to get the better of her colleagues. It was all over in a few moments. The tigers were literally blown to pieces by the terrific blast of energy and four ragged and scratched Crusaders reeled towards the Amazon as she stood waiting.

"Nice work," Abna complimented her, breathing hard. "I thought we were finished that time. We didn't even get a chance to use our guns."

"Any of you hurt?" the Amazon asked briefly, and the others shook their heads as they pulled the torn parts of their space-tights together.

"Nothing that can't soon be fixed," Viona responded. "We'd better get to that 'plane before somebody starts releasing a horde of mastodons or sonething on top of us."

"And none of that would have happened but for me," Thania said bitterly. "I just couldn't help it. I haven't got your nerve—"

"Forget it," the Amazon said, picking up the fallen proton guns and handing them over. "It was a natural reaction for a young girl. Now let's be on our way."

She set the example by starting to move swiftly towards the giant idol, which formed part of the gateway ahead. As she went, the others immediately behind her, the loudspeaker voice burst into fresh life again.

"You are not without courage and strength, my friends. It was a pity indeed that such skill and power should only have me for a spectator. That was worthy of a large audience—"

"I don't know who's talking, but ignore it," the Amazon said, as Abna caught up with her. "What we want is that 'plane—then we'll get out of here as fast as we can go. My fear is that we'll be stopped again yet."

By this time she had reached the gateway. She paused for a moment and, with the others, stood looking up at the idol's hideous face—then just as quickly her mind snapped back to the matter on hand.

"Give me a hand up," she ordered briefly, and Abna obeyed, swinging her up to his vast shoulders. From them she leapt upwards and gripped the top of the gateway arch tightly. Muscular strength did the rest.

Then she turned and helped the others up one by one. As she did so she wondered what the unseen observer was doing—probably plotting some new villainy to hinder them, or perhaps he was elsewhere, relying on the fact that as far as he knew the five could not escape from the arena.

In this he was to be disappointed. Once at the top of the gateway the Crusaders dropped immediately to the other side, and though they never paused in their advance to the 'plane they kept their guns ready and were ever watchful of trouble materializing.

They seemed however to be wrong. Despite the fact that it was full daylight now, and that the area surrounding the 'plane was within sight of the endless terraces of houses, there was no sign of action, perhaps because it was too early in the morning. Or, at a distance, people who might be watching assumed the five were concerned with normal duties in the arena.

"Look neither right nor left," the Amazon counseled, as they dropped to the big open space. "We want that 'plane, and if anybody tries to stop us—Well, it'll be too bad for them!"

It was as well she gave the advice for as they came near to the 'plane several oddly-uniformed men came out of one of the buildings. Their first appearance was casual enough, talking amongst themselves, then they stared blankly at the Crusaders. The pause only lasted for fractional seconds then evidently guessing what was intended they tugged weapons from their uniform belts and quickly advanced, one of them shouting as he ran.

"Hey, what are you doing? Stop! Stop I say!"

To add point to his words he fired his weapon. A sizzling stream of fire shot across the Amazon's path, which was all that was needed to release her quick temper into full action.

She wheeled, firing her own proton-gun at the same time—and this time with a lightning flick of the wrist she twirled the nozzle to full width. Instantly there was a terrific blast of flame and a numbing shock wave from directly in front of the running men. They were none of them was hurt but they did go stumbling head over heels into a deep, smoking pit which had been gouged in the earth.

"That'll settle 'em," the Amazon grinned. "Right—let's get a move on!"

In a matter of seconds, whilst the bewildered men struggled to disentangle themselves from the pit, the five Crusaders reached the 'plane and dived through its open airlock. The Amazon hurried to the control board studying the layout. Then she glanced quickly out of the window.

Other men were appearing now on the big landing space, some of them in fast-moving vehicles—and all were converging towards the 'plane. Evidently the general alarm had been raised.

"I'll take a gamble in this thing," the Amazon said, as the others glanced at her anxiously. "If we can get into the air I'll figure the rest out when we're there."

Since all 'planes must, she reasoned, have a similar system of control she risked pressing a bright red button—and instantly there was a soft humming which proclaimed an engine had come to life somewhere. After that she pulled over a lever marked '1' and hoped for the best. Certainly she got a result—almost too much of one for comfort!

The 'plane shot almost vertically into the air and at a velocity which would have done credit to any spaceship! The altimeter needle on the dashboard sailed to 1,000 and then 2,000 feet before the Amazon's frantic ministrations suddenly checked the upward climb. The 'plane whizzed round in a wide arc and then slackened speed as the Amazon adjusted what was evidently the power-lever to half. Then she turned and smiled rather sheepishly at Abna as he closed the airlock. He looked at her rather grimly.

"Aerobatics, at this time, are not required," he reminded her.

"Sorry. I'm not quite sure of the controls. Anyway, I think we'll be all right now."

Apparently they were for the 'plane kept flying on even keel, high over the southern England countryside. The view of buildings perched on terraces became a continuous thing, stretching over the countryside without a break and involving even London, which so far as being capital of the country was concerned, seemed no longer to exist. Always there were the buildings on terraces, with an occasional variation as a larger outcropping of edifices came into view. Or, here and there, there was a gigantic road, but with very few vehicles in sight at this early hour in the morning. Aircraft there seemed to be in plenty, and always fortunately at a distance. By and large, it was evident as the 'plane flew on that England had become completely transformed.

At the border between England and Scotland the ground pattern 2,000 feet below changed. The terraced buildings became less frequent, and finally ceased as the 'plane raced on into the Scottish Highlands. Down below, things had a more normal appearance—a crofter's cottage here and there, or agricultural outbuildings; and then presently signs of commercialism once again as a city, completely foreign to the Crusaders, loomed up towards the north of Scotland. This appeared to be quite normal even if it was vastly advanced on the old days. Certainly there was nothing of the Romanesque atmosphere about it.

"Well, I certainly don't understand it," the Amazon confessed at last, pondering as she gazed below. "What ought we to do? Go and see if Europe looks the same, or cross the Atlantic and have a look at America and the rest of the world?"

"I rather think," Abna said, turning from his own observation window, "that there isn't going to be the chance to do either. We're on the verge of being intercepted. Take a look for yourselves."

At that, the rest of the party joined Abna and the Amazon round the windows, gazing in some dismay at the sight of half a dozen airplanes, not unlike the one they had commandeered, sweeping upwards quickly from the depths of the huge, sprawling city below. The Amazon turned to make quick alterations on the switchboard, but Abna caught her arm.

"No, Vi—wait a minute. They've got the whip hand of us this time. They know what weapons they've got whereas we don't even know where to begin in this ship. Better let them come and sort it out from there. We've still got proton-guns to deal out plenty of grief, if need be."

The Amazon hesitated, plainly undecided; then with a grim face she cut down the aircraft's speed as the six intercepting planes formed in a decisive line ahead... Then at a suddenly winking signal light on the nearby instrument board Abna turned quickly and switched on the radio equipment. In a moment or two a voice became audible—authoritative and with a distinct Scots burr.

"...beyond prescribed sky territory. You are ordered to return whence you came." There was a pause and then the voice repeated itself. "Your aircraft is beyond the prescribed territory. You are ordered to return whence you came."

Abna switched on the microphone and spoke briefly: "We have no wish to return. We would prefer to converse with you."

Pause. The Amazon raised an eyebrow but she did not question Abna's motives. She well realized he knew what he was doing.

"Who are you?" came the Scots voice. "Are you not from Railstrom, or some part thereof?"

"Railstrom?" Abna repeated in surprise. "I never heard of it."

"That is hard to believe. It is the only city in this country, apart from our own, and your 'plane has obviously come from there and is violating our air space."

"I take it," Abna said, "that you are referring to the city which looks as though it has become Rome? The one with a coliseum at its southern boundary."

"Exactly—the city of Railstrom… Now do as you are ordered and return there immediately, otherwise as flight-leader of this unit I will not be responsible for what might happen to you."

"It would appear that we are at cross-purposes," Abna said grimly. "I am but one of five people aboard this plane, and none of us ever heard of Railstrom until you mentioned it. We are bent on escaping from there. Nor do we know anything about this city, which we see below us in the Scottish Highlands—"

"Did you say 'Scottish'?" There was uncertainty in the other's voice. "Scotland has not even existed for generations! Who exactly are you if you are not from Railstrom?"

"We are known as the Cosmic Crusaders. We would not be on Earth at all if a trick hadn't snared us here!"

At the other end there was something that sounded suspiciously like a gasp; then there followed a hurried but unintelligible conversation with somebody else. At length the voice spoke clearly again.

"Most certainly there has been a misunderstanding somewhere. Please accept our profound apologies. If you will place yourselves in our care we will escort you to Lanatock—that is the city below you."

"You mean we're prisoners?" Abna demanded.

"Anything but it, my friend. Guests—and very honored guests. Your coming has been awaited, but we never expected you to arrive in this fashion."

With that he switched off, and wondering vaguely what was to happen next, the five stood watching as the six attendant fliers swept round gracefully and then began to dive down toward the city of Lanatock. The Amazon resumed her former role of pilot and began to follow swiftly behind them.

"What do you think is going on?" Viona questioned, frowning. "Why should we be honored guests all of a sudden? It's the first time it's happened in all our adventures—and it doesn't make sense."

"Why doesn't it?" Mexone asked. "Why should everybody always be enemies? Why should we always be suspected of villainous intent when all we're trying to do is help people?"

Viona shrugged. "I'm merely remembering what's happened to us. We've been dragged from the Milky Way and nearly killed on Mercury—albeit unintentionally perhaps, as far as Mercury's concerned—and then we're told we're expected and are honored guests. The circumstances don't match up."

"They very rarely do in the kind of life we lead," Abna remarked. "Anyway, we'll soon find out what it's all about, I've no doubt. And let's hope there'll be a meal laid on. It occurs to me that I'm mighty hungry."

The others nodded in sympathy with his feelings, then turned to watch the scene below as they came ever nearer Lanatock. It was a bigger city than they had imagined, stretching for untold miles of suburbs in a northerly direction; but the main hub of the city seemed to be a group of massively tall buildings with extensive landing fields toward which they were now descending with their escort.

In another moment or two they had reached them. The Amazon switched off the power, pulled back the airlock door, and then stood waiting and watching as the escort planes each disgorged a party of men, smartly uniformed, who wasted no time in hurrying over to the Crusaders' vessel. Finally, the one who was presumably the leader paused outside the airlock and stood looking up to where the Amazon and the others had congregated.

He was by no means a bad-looking man, with humorous blue eyes and the lean features of a typical Scot.

"Greetings," he said, saluting smartly. "I am he who was talking to you over the radio—Flight-Leader Manley at your service. I said then, and I say again, that you are very honored guests."

"Perhaps," the Amazon said. "You will be kind enough to direct us to somebody in authority?"

"That is exactly my intention—if you will follow me?"

The Crusaders, convinced by now that for the present at least all was well, did not waste any more time. They stepped through the airlock and then followed Flight-Leader Manley as he walked away from his men and across the landing strip. The men watched, interested—then after a short walk Manley led the way into one of the many buildings around the airfield. A short walk up a narrow passage brought him to a door marked PRIVATE. He knocked sharply, then threw the door open wide as a voice bade him come in.

"Presenting the Cosmic Crusaders, sir," he announced, saluting and then standing to one side. "The party for whom General Milford has been waiting."

The middle-aged man at the desk in the center of the file-filled room looked up in surprise. His gaze shifted to the Crusaders as they entered.

"The Cosmic Crusaders?" he repeated, plainly amazed. "But I was under the impression…" He meditated, then: "I was under the impression that you had died, quite accidentally, on Mercury."

"I trust," Abna said coldly, "that that was not the intention."

"Good heavens, no! Mischance—miscalculation, resulted in you being flung on Mercury…" The man at the desk seemed to take a hold of himself and then went on, "Believe me when I say that I am more than delighted that you live. It is not my province to tell you why we need you so desperately; that is our ruler's business—General Milford—and it is him whom you must see."

"General Milford is the ruler?" the Amazon repeated. "Do you mean ruler of the world, or this particular country?"

"That is not an easy question to answer." The man at the desk hesitated for a moment. "I would prefer to leave it to General Milford himself to explain… Flight-Leader!"

"Sir?"

"Make arrangements for these good friends of ours to be transported immediately to General Milford's headquarters. I will advise him by radio that they are on their way."

"Very good, sir."

The Flight-Leader turned and left and the man at the desk relaxed a little and smiled.

"Forgive me for being so mysterious," he said. "You see, I have not got absolute authority in this matter. It is entirely up to the General… Do be seated, my friends, and I will have refreshments brought to you whilst you are waiting."

CHAPTER 4

Earth Divided

In a matter of half an hour later, pleasantly refreshed with wholesome Earthly food and drink—of which they partook in a quiet anteroom—the five still much-puzzled Crusaders were whisked away on the final stage of their journey. As before it was accomplished by plane, with only the Flight-Leader at the controls, and none of his men.

The course of the journey surprised the Crusaders not a little. They had expected rapid transportation to some big building somewhere else in the city—so they were astonished when the city of Lanatock was rapidly left behind and the plane flew over desolate Scottish mountain heights, never pausing until the extreme north tip of Scotland was reached—a mountainous terrain with not a single habitation in sight. Here, in the remoteness, the 'plane began to descend.

"Is this to be the end of our journey?" the Amazon asked in surprise, and the Flight-Leader nodded.

"The headquarters of General Milford, Amazon. Don't assume too much from the topography below. It is extremely well camouflaged."

The truth of this became evident in a moment or two as the 'plane swept down to apparently bare rock—only it proved to be nothing of the kind. Some photo-electric-cell device was obviously released as the 'plane crossed an activating beam for, suddenly, the rocky ground opened up into a huge canyon—easily capable of taking the 'plane's size, and a good many more aircraft as well, probably.

Quite unconcerned, Manley drove on steadily, still directing the 'plane downwards until it came finally into a tunnel. Darkness dropped after a moment, but a series of twinkling lights on the control panel were enough to enable Manley to find his course—for after about 20 minutes of steady flight through the dark, there was a growing suggestion of grayness, which merged rapidly into brilliance as they entered a titanic cavern festooned with lights. Here the 'plane dropped to the cavern floor and became still.

"Our journey is at an end," Manley remarked, switching off the engine. "The entrance to this underworld sealed itself after we had entered and we are now about a mile below ground. You will have gathered…" He opened the airlock. "You will have gathered that General Milford and his staff have taken every precaution."

"Obviously," the Amazon assented. "But I am led to ask what the precautions are for. Of whom is General Milford afraid?"

"The Pagans," Manley said seriously; then without explaining himself further he indicated the airlock. "If you will all come with me?"

The five showed no hesitation. They followed the Flight-Leader out of the 'plane to the cavern floor, then walked behind him as he matched towards many of the buildings nearby. They had a Governmental look about them—composed of dull gray, uninteresting looking metal and brightly lighted through the windows. There were about fifty of these buildings all linked together and forming a circle about the center of the cavern floor. Judging from the sound coming from some of them, big engines were at work.

The puzzled five again asked themselves what it was all about. Why such elaborate precautions in the depths of the Earth? Why this little city with every aspect of modernity and advanced engineering tucked away in remote northern Scotland? Who were the Pagans? Perhaps something to do with the Romanesque city, the Coliseum, and the wild animals…?

Presently, still a little way ahead, Manley led the way into one of the buildings and in the hallway two soldiers in uniform, with a strange insignia on their breasts, sprang to attention—then they relaxed again as they beheld the Flight-Leader. He saluted, the men stood back, and the Crusaders went on their way down a long metal passage, its walls lined with ribbons of flickerless yet oddly unhurtful light. White light, strangely intense.

"Believe it or not," the Amazon murmured, as Abna walked beside her, "I think this is cold light." She stretched out her hand toward the ice-cold tube near to her. "I thought as much outside when I saw the clusters in the cavern roof. Now I'm sure of it. Though we ourselves solved the secret of cold light ages ago, it's a new achievement for Earth. Shows the evolution of intelligence since we left."

Abna nodded but he had no chance to say much as, with Manley, they crossed a hidden photoelectric beam and a door opened sharply in front of them. They were in yet another chamber, surrounded by switch panels, in the center of which was a very ordinary-looking office desk before which sat a solitary man. He was busily writing.

"The Cosmic Crusaders, General," Manley said, and at that the solitary man looked up, obviously of high rank to judge from the host of decorations and emblems on his uniform.

"Thank you, Flight-Leader." His voice was measured and deep. "You may retire."

Manley retreated backwards with an enormous amount of formality, saluted, and then went out and closed the door. At that, General Milford noticeably relaxed and got to his feet, smiling. He was a massively built man, not very much short of Abna's own seven-foot height. His face was immediately impressive—craggy and rugged beyond the average, and yet somehow genial, as though he were both a man of iron will and spiritual power.

"My friends," he said quietly, coming forward and shaking hands. "You have no idea what this means to me—to everybody in fact. To have found you at last…" He indicated the various light chairs scattered about the room. "Please be seated. You would like some refreshment, perhaps?"

"Thank you, no," the Amazon responded, sitting down. "That was attended to before we left for here. We are concerned with a more vital matter. Why are we here? Why were we virtually abducted back to Earth?"

"For that," General Milford said, "I must offer you all a complete and unqualified apology." He sat down again at the chair at his desk. "There was no other way of contacting you."

"No other way?" Abna repeated, and raised his eyebrows. "I grant you that radio communication would have been difficult—even impossible—at our vast distance away, but surely there was a better method than tricking us from our vessel?"

"Unfortunately, there was not. Let me begin from the beginning and explain afterwards why you are needed here. First, there arose the necessity of contacting you. Using hyperspatial principles, we made magnetic instruments sensitive enough to give us a reading of your distance away—rather like your own aura compass, which once the aura of a person is known, can determine their presence and approximate distance at any known point in the universe. Only our device gave a reading on your Ultra's position, not yourselves. It showed us where you were and the huge distance involved. We had hoped for that, knowing from records that the Ultra has a magnetic prow."

"Records?" the Amazon repeated, and Milford nodded.

"Certainly. There are records of your history—your birth, prowess, marriage, and so on, and the construction of your Ultra. Records also of your comings and goings from this Earth. Time and again by your uncanny scientific knowledge and physical strength you have saved this world from ruin—and other worlds too. To cut a long story short, we knew from the records that your Ultra has a magnetic prow, which ought to give a directional pull on a sufficiently sensitive instrument. Such an instrument was built by our best scientists and your position was determined."

"Then?" the Amazon questioned.

"Then, unfortunately, we came up against a problem. We could not find any astronaut willing to make the enormous journey to contact you. Our spacemen just shied at it. Partly because of the rigors involved at terrific velocities, and also—I fancy—because many of them did not believe that you could—or would—help us even if the journey were attempted. That such a trip could be made and the traveler still survive you have proved for yourselves—but then we had to remember your super-human qualities and it was felt that no normal spaceman could live through the journey… So we evolved a strategy."

This time the five did not respond. They sat waiting for the next, their faces somewhat grim. And General Milford continued:

"We sent a ship, somewhat on the design of your own Ultra, and set its course by super computers. It was devised to travel many times faster than light so as to hurdle the enormous distance within reasonable time instead of taking several lifetimes. Also, all the controls and power plant were indestructibly sealed so as to prevent them being touched or the course interfered with. Our reasoning was that, curious as to the nature of the ship, you would board it to investigate. Then the trap would close, so to speak, and willy-nilly you would be brought back to Earth. Telescopic observation was kept on you and eventually the ship was sighted, but due to a hair-degree error in our calculations the vessel overshot the Earth's orbit and was last seen hurtling towards Mercury. We gave you up for lost, realizing that even if we flew ships out to you with all speed we would never be in time.

"Then," Milford finished in amazement, "you suddenly appeared here. Just *how* we don't know. Telescopic watch had been withdrawn, of course, but our alarms—set for a ship the size of the Ultra—never signaled anything. You were simply—here!"

"The ship in which we came from Mercury is only half its original size—or rather was," the Amazon said. "It now lies at the bottom of the sea…" Briefly she explained the circumstances and then added, "You arranged it so that our Ultra, an immensely valuable and indeed dangerous vessel in the wrong hands, was left behind in the First Galaxy. Whilst admitting that considerable scientific skill and not a little psychology was used to contact us, why did you leave our ship behind? It could have followed the other ship, chained to it by the law of mass, had it been allowed to."

"Until you neared Earth it could have done," Milford agreed. "Then it might have caught up with the first machine and caused no end of trouble. Further we could not risk a second machine, as its weight would have set our calculations out of order. According to our arrangement, it was better to cast the Ultra free."

"Not a very bright idea," the Amazon said, still uncompromising. "You'd understand what I mean if you knew what terrible weapons have been left behind on our vessel, machines which in the hands of wandering and clever scientists could destroy the very universe."

There was silence for a moment then rather uncomfortably General Milford said:

"We still have our detector in action to show where your vessel is in the First Galaxy. Once you have conferred on us the favor of completing the mission we have set for you, you can return to your Ultra, with our devout thanks for your help."

"That seems fair enough," Abna remarked, before the Amazon could speak. "Perhaps you'd better explain to us why you've gone to such trouble to find us?"

"I have called on you, Amazon, in particular," Milford said, "because Earth is your native planet, is it not, and I felt that you above all others would wish to save it from catastrophe."

"What kind of catastrophe? You seem pretty well organized scientifically, and certainly you are well protected down here. What is this something you can't handle?"

"Barbarity, allied to scientific power, which has divided the world into two camps. It began many generations ago as a cold war, as it was popularly called. Today it is something different—an insidious poison which is slowly engulfing the whole world. This poison I speak of is a far more dangerous and important than the occasional flarings of open warfare which occur."

The Amazon shrugged and glanced in bewilderment at the others. She said: "I still do not understand."

The General leaned forward on his desk. "On the one hand we have the Normals—our name for millions like myself, and by reason of votes and general confidence I have become their leader. We cover roughly one-half of the Earth's surface. On the other hand we have the Pagans, with their own ruler, filling the other half of this planet. They have disavowed everything and deliberately abandoned all the decent ways and chivalries that make a social order possible. They live by science, and cruelty, and so steeped have they become in paganism that they worship an idol, a monstrous thing of—"

"We've seen it—or rather a replica," the Amazon interrupted. "Designed to form a gateway to a wild animal arena."

"Then on that score I do not need to explain further. From the appearance of the idol you can glean some idea what kind of minds the Pagans have."

"Completely," the Amazon assented: and Milford continued:

"By every known means, day and night, using every possible method, the Pagans have built up their doctrine of power through cruelty. They comprise a vast and godless horde who threaten to exterminate us, and engulf the world in moral darkness. Once in their clutches it is impossible to defy them; they force their propaganda down our throats incessantly, by radio, television, and every other modern means. To defy them means death or torture—and maybe both."

The Amazon said: "There have been similar outbreaks of despotism in the world before."

"True; but never on a scale like this! Or inflicted with such cold, inhuman ferocity. Day by day we see people influenced to join the ranks of the Pagans, and those who afterwards think they have made a mistake, and dare to say so, usually end up in the Coliseum-like arena as playthings for the wild animals."

"The same one that we crossed, I suppose," the Amazon said. "I have told you already how we—"

"Yes, the same," Milford confirmed. "It is one of the largest in Railstrom, though there are others in different parts of the world. There, twice a week, the Pagan leaders and general populace assemble to enjoy the torment and destruction of those whom they consider disloyal."

"Isn't that rather a strange state of affairs?" Viona put in. "A race obviously scientific in progress and outlook indulging in inquisitions as the Romans did. There was some excuse for the Romans, perhaps; they hadn't got minds above their cruel way of life; but surely in this advanced age it doesn't—"

"I'm afraid it does," Milford interrupted. "There is an evil side to almost every man and woman. Give it full liberty and withdraw all penalties from indulging it, and the result is barbarism and scientific intelligence wedded together. The Pagans' cruelty in the arena has often been criticized by the Normals, but the Pagans say that no scientific villainy devised ever equals the callousness of the arena. Man and beast against each other adds up to a supposed fighting chance—but of course there is none." General Milford got up and began to move restlessly. "So, my friends, you see the terrible state of affairs which has come to Earth. Casting around for somebody to help crush this vicious tide and restore to the world the normal way of life, our thoughts turned to you—the Cosmic Crusaders, liberators of the crushed and uninitiated. I felt I must contact you, by any means I could. And by the way I expected only three of you, since three left Earth. Five is a surprise,"

"Thania and Mexone joined us from their own worlds during our travels," the Amazon replied. "But you needn't fear that they are any the less strong or intelligent than Abna, Viona and myself. Scientific surgery has taken care of that..." Then as she apparently decided to become amenable to the situation, the Amazon said:

"You want us to put this world—a world divided—back to normal and destroy the power of the Pagans? Is that it?"

"That's it," Milford said quietly.

CHAPTER 5

Ultimatum

"That's a pretty tall order," the Amazon said, after a moment. "Even more so when we have only a few proton guns and instruments in our belts… Have you not done anything for yourselves? Obviously your science is anything but undeveloped."

"Our science and that of the Pagans is of about the same order. Our science grew up together, in fact, through the generations—and since the cleavage of ideals they have remained about equal. But unfortunately there is a snag."

"And it is?" Abna asked.

"Just this. Our defenses are never prepared for the uses to which the Pagans put their scientific knowledge—never prepared for their underhand ways and ruthless misuse of power: They know no law and no restraint. For that reason most of our main science is underground here and I am at the nerve-center of it all. Behold the switchboards!"

The Amazon nodded her blonde head as Milford indicated them. Then she asked a question:

"How do these Pagans gain ground? Is it by warlike methods, threats, propaganda by radio, television, and so forth, before which the Normals fall?"

"That is the procedure in the main. The Pagans have immensely powerful radio-television stations, which can reach all over the world, night and day. With television and radio as their allies, the Pagans reiterate a gospel of violence and power. It is inevitable that a vast majority of Normals, lured by false promises, must fall. Some embrace the new doctrine and become virtual slaves. Others, as I have said, disclaim it—and die."

"I wonder," the Amazon mused, "why we were allowed to get so far across that arena in Railstrom before somebody thought of turning wilds animals loose on us?"

Milford smiled cynically. "A typical Pagan trick, Amazon. It must have been obvious to the watcher with the voice that you were not Pagans: your very attire would betray that fact. He must have realized that you had strayed into the arena for some reason, so he waited until he thought you could not escape and then he turned the tigers loose upon you. The biggest shock must have come when you fought them and escaped."

"Yes, that must have been it." The Amazon nodded to herself; then she looked questioningly at the others. "Well, what do we do? Accept this challenge and try to put things right?"

"After traveling across countless light years we could hardly refuse," Abna responded, and at that the Amazon nodded quick agreement. It was plain from the expression on her beautiful face that she was more than ready to pit her wits and scientific knowledge against those who had made a bedlam of her home planet. She turned back to the General again as he sat anxiously waiting.

"We'll do our best," she said quietly, "but only on the understanding that we handle the campaign in our own way and are given all the outside help we need. It won't be easy because this 'persuasive cancer' seems to have spread so far... There is also something else. When the campaign is over we are to have every facility for getting back to our Ultra."

"Both requests are willingly granted," Milford said promptly. "I realize the dangers of this undertaking but I am perfectly confident that you can put things right." He rose to his feet and gave a serious smile. "Think yourselves fortunate that you approached Earth in half a ship, my friends. A full sized one might easily have been spotted by the pagans and promptly shot down. In that, at least, fortune favored us. Now—" He became suddenly decisive, "Regarding your headquarters. You can have every facility down here if that will do. At least you will not be exposed to needless danger."

"It should do admirably," the Amazon agreed. "The sooner we can retire to our quarters and formulate plans, the better."

"I will make immediate arrangements for you to be conducted," the General said, pressing a bell-push. "Down here, as I have said, you are perfectly safe. I have mentioned that at times there are flarings of war from the Pagans: when this happens they use everything they've got, including nuclear explosives. In these depths we are safe, protected by the tons of rock and every explosive repellant known to science. The Pagans would dearly love to smash these headquarters of mine but so far they have had no success—nor will they."

Milford paused as a guard came in and saluted smartly. "Your orders, sir?"

"Conduct these five to Section B-2, guard, the quarters which have been specifically assigned to them." And as the Crusaders turned to go Milford added, "I will be constantly in touch with you, and you with me. If you want anything, no matter how trivial, let me know. In regard to your personal comforts, you will find a staff of servants ready to attend to you."

The Amazon nodded her thanks and then led the way to the door. When she got there she paused and looked back with a faint smile.

"Better be prepared for trouble in various forms, General," she said. "My instincts tell me that there's trouble coming—plenty of it. And I am very seldom wrong!"

* * * *

In the quarters assigned to them the Crusaders found they had every comfort, and it was a decided change for them to have everything earthly and immediately understandable, with none of the riddles that had usually attended domicile on a distant planet.

Their moves were swift and to the point. Since it was obvious that the main power of the Pagans—apart from actual weapons—relied on their radio and television, the Amazon gave immediate orders through General Milford for all stations to be jammed. True, it meant that all over the world the Normals were unable to receive radio or television, but at least it had the advantage that they could not be influenced by propaganda either. Only one station was left un-jammed—the Central Receiving Station in Milford's headquarters. Here, one man alone received and recorded all the information as he got it. Most of it followed the usual pattern, until about a week later there was a change—urgent enough for the five Crusaders to be immediately summoned to General Milford's headquarters.

"I am afraid," he said grimly, when he had greeted them, "that we are in for trouble as you prophesied, Amazon. The Pagans have finally awakened to the fact that their broadcasts are jammed and that you—the Cosmic Crusaders—are responsible for it. Listen to this message from the leader of the Pagans, which was recorded."

The General switched on the recorder and the five listened in silence, their expressions becoming grimmer as time passed.

"It has come to our notice, General Milford, that instead of accepting the progress of our doctrine as a natural process of advancement, you have decided to try and stop it. You probably feel confident because you have the backing of those five scientific upstarts from outer space—the Cosmic Crusaders as they call themselves. I am informed that they are here on Earth and indeed were right in our clutches, until the guard of the Railstrom arena allowed them to escape. He has since suffered death for his negligence, after he had revealed the facts to us…"

Milford gave a hard glance. "That's the kind of thing they do—no trial, no anything. Instant execution. Then they—"

The message resumed: "The jamming of radio and television is undoubtedly the work of the Cosmic Crusaders, but we are not so foolish as to think that you have not left a station open somewhere and through it we send this message, confident that it will reach you. Take great heed of what we say… We shall not tolerate interference in our plans, either from you or these five scientific super beings whom you mistakenly imagine can help you… Here is an ultimatum: The five Crusaders will be handed over to us in Railstrom, under a guard of truce, which you shall supply, by midnight tonight. If you fail to do this, five unnamed towns—one for each Crusader—will be blasted from the Earth! You can regard it as a reprisal measure, and if after that if there is still no compliance with our demands, another five towns and their populations will be destroyed.

And so on, each day, until you see sense. Heed the warning well. That is all."

There was a click and the message ceased. The Amazon stirred a little in her chair. Milford looked across at her.

"In other words, open warfare," he said curtly. "The occasional sallies which have taken place up to now will fade into nothing before this new threat. Five unnamed towns will be certainly obliterated by nuclear power if the demand is not complied with."

"You don't suggest we hand ourselves over, do you?" Viona demanded.

"No—of course not." Milford shifted uncomfortably. "The position is an awkward one. The destruction of five towns will involve the death and injury of thousands of people. The Normals will cry out for a surrender before they too are smashed down—and in that way the Pagans win. I did warn you of their brutality and power."

"Obviously," the Amazon said, with a significant glance at Viona, "there is only one solution to the problem. We shall have to do as the Pagans ask. If we don't, we will indirectly be the slayers of thousands, which is totally against our principles."

Milford looked his astonishment. "You're joking, of course?"

"Not at all. I rarely joke, as Abna will tell you. I believe only in cold logic and ruthless action. Jokes are a waste of time."

"But—" Milford looked dismayed. "What becomes of the campaign, the very thing for which you're here?"

"That," the Amazon mused, "will have to be considered very carefully. We have until midnight—a matter of some 14 hours. We have come to important decisions in far less time than that, and we are going to do so again. The campaign will go on—have no fear of that. Once we are in the hands of the Pagans, despite the danger to ourselves, we will automatically reduce a good deal of surveillance."

"Maybe," the General responded, in obvious irritation, "but what other plans have you? As far as I can see you are out of the picture the moment the Pagans have their hands on you—and I may as well tell you I won't allow you to sacrifice yourselves without putting up a fight."

The Amazon's expressions changed a little. "Be sure of one thing, General, you can't put up a fight against people like this and win it. And without the Ultra, our most valuable possession, neither can we. But, there are other ways, which may demand a good deal of careful planning. With your permission I would like to discuss matters with my colleagues."

"Whatever you wish, Amazon. You are in complete charge."

"Right… Inform the head of the Pagans by radio that his demand will be acceded to—that my companions and I will present ourselves, under a guard of truce, at midnight tonight. That ought to ward off the threatened attack on five unnamed towns."

"And ensure your death warrants." Milford looked from one to the other. "That is the part I don't like."

The Amazon said: "Leave us to worry over that, General, and do your part. Come with me, the rest of you: we have much to discuss."

With that the Amazon nodded a leave-taking to the General and led the way out of the office. The others followed her, puzzled and not at all at ease. When she finally gained the main room of their own quarters they looked at her with grim faces.

"Pretty rash promises, Vi," Abna said quietly, speaking

for all of them. "Even though I'm pretty sure you had good reason for making them."

"No other reason than to save the lives of the hapless people in five unnamed towns," the Amazon shrugged. "As to the Pagans, they will do their utmost, no doubt, but we're not exactly amateurs at getting out of tight corners... However, I have another plan which, if it works, ought to bring the Pagans to their knees."

"We're listening," Mexone said, without any great enthusiasm.

The Amazon began moving slowly, driving her right fist into her left palm to emphasize the statement that followed.

"As I see it, according to Milford himself, the Pagans have the whip hand through their ruthlessness and knowledge of science. But it is a science limited to Earth and wielded with merciless power. How would they react to a menace conceived in outer space against which they have no defense? They'd crumble in a moment. We are used to conceiving weapons in space, with no planetary foundation: The Pagans are not. Therein may lie our victory over them."

"What have you in mind?" Abna asked quietly.

"A burning glass," the Amazon replied. "And it is the remembrance of the conditions we found on Mercury that brings it to mind."

"How do you mean—a burning glass?" Thania asked at last.

"I mean a glass—a lens—the diameter of Mercury and balanced in space. A glass which will gather the heat waves of the sun and concentrate them down through the Earth's atmosphere, when of course they will take on their normal property of unbearable heat. A shaft of heat so furiously hot that it will melt the toughest metal in a moment. Imagine it concentrated on a city. Everything would catch fire instantly and nothing would remain but a smoking wilderness."

"A burning glass…" Viona repeated, musing. "But that's impossible. We'll be in the hands of the Pagans by midnight, and a job such as you are suggesting would take weeks, or longer—granting the tools were at hand to do it, which they aren't."

"I'll explain again," the Amazon said, with quiet deliberation. "On Mercury, in the molten state, are all the ingredients for fashioning a gigantic lens, which can afterwards be hardened by moving the lens to the night side of the planet. The planet has the necessary potash, soda, lime, magnesia, lead and so forth, and the matter of the grinding and polishing can be done afterwards by ordinary laboratory methods, which General Milford will supply as needed. Imagine then, a lens approximately as wide as Mercury when it is finished. As for the rest, that will be a matter of maneuver and applied mathematics to determine where the lens shall concentrate the sun's power. To move the lens in free space will not be a difficult task."

"I grant you all that," Abna said, "but you are ignoring the most important part. We shan't be there to perform this scientific miracle."

"Not in person," the Amazon agreed, "but there are ways round that too, which from here on until we leave for Railstrom must be our primary consideration. I mean," she added, "duplicates of ourselves."

Abna smiled rather regretfully. "I'm afraid you're pipe-dreaming, Vi. Though we can certainly create duplicates of ourselves, and have done it before many a time, we can't do it without the material to work on. That's far away in the Ultra, in the Milky Way. You know that."

"True," the Amazon agreed, "but I also know that you and I, Abna, have good enough memories to make the duplicating machines on the spot, with General Milford to supply the materials and the labor for the job. Given the stuff and armies of workers, the duplicating machines could be made within six hours. Do that, and we have cleared the first hurdle."

Thania, who had been listening intently, asked a question:

"Apart from duplicating ourselves—which is a scientific miracle in itself—why is it necessary? Can't you give instructions to General Milford's men as to what to do?"

The Amazon shook her blonde head. "It just wouldn't do. They would not be able to stand the terrible conditions of Mercury's sunward side for the long time required, and again—being human—they might easily betray information to spies as to what they were doing. Duplicates, on the other hand, can suffer any amount of rigors and remain unmoved, and they'd carry out our orders to the letter once the instructions were electronically imprinted on their synthetic brains. In other words, they will be us, and doing as we would, unmoved by a single circumstance. We ourselves, leaving the real work to our duplicates, will tackle whatever the Pagans confront us with."

There was silence for a moment. As usual, any plan devised by the Golden Amazon was super-scientific to the nth degree, and made light of the formidable dangers that actually existed.

"Assuming all this to be possible," Viona said presently, "what precisely do you intend—including the possibility that we may be dead and unable to see what takes place?"

"We shan't be dead," the Amazon retorted. "We've survived too many things in our experience to allow the Pagans to put the finishing touch. As to my intentions—once the lens is completed—which will obviously be on Mercury—it will be projected into space to a point determined by mathematics, a point where it will be ideally suited to train the concentrated rays of the sun through it and to the Earth, approximately 100 million miles away. Control of it will be handled from Mercury itself. Naturally, wherever the concentrated rays touch there will be terrific conflagration. On the chance that there is nothing we can do to save ourselves from the Pagans we will leave orders with General Milford, the logical person since he's head of the Normals. In other words, he will tell the Pagans that unless their depredations cease, unless they come into line with the rest of the sane folk in the world, he will unleash upon them scientific violence of a character they have never known… A legacy from the Cosmic Crusaders."

"Which the Pagans will treat with contempt!" Viona sighed. "You know the kind of people they are."

"Until, one by one, their cities vanish in smoke and flame," the Amazon retorted. "They will of course discover in double quick time what is causing the trouble, and will probably launch armadas into space to destroy the lens—but long before they get to it they will be met by a shaft of unbearable fire which will liquidate them. It is the only weapon we have with no Ultra to aid us, but it's formidable just the same."

"It's formidable all right," Abna agreed. "And typical of you, Vi. Granting that we ever succeed in making such a weapon—or rather that our potential duplicates do—aren't we rather defeating our own ends as upholders of law and order? A weapon like that, which can fry whole populations in an instant of time, is far ahead of anything nuclear, and certainly more painful in its method of extermination than, say, the Zero-amplifier machine on our lost Ultra."

"I am hoping," the Amazon said, "that the threats made will not have to be carried out. Maybe the destruction of something unimportant by a shaft of heat from outer space will do the trick and show that it is not a joke. If it doesn't, then rather than see the whole world finally engulfed by these dictators it may be necessary to give a practical demonstration."

"Certainly these Pagans, even with their vaunted knowledge of science, won't be able to fight a thing like that," Mexone said, after a moment. "Nuclear warfare and Earthly science is something they can understand and probably defeat, but a solar lens in space ought to have them licked. That is of a scientific order that isn't up their street."

"Exactly." As usual, with her mind decided on a plan, the Amazon wasted no time in putting it into effect. Her voice became sharply decisive. "We have an enormous lot to do before we hand ourselves over to the Pagans, so we'd better get started… Abna, use your memory to help me think of a design of those duplicating machines. Viona, work out the necessary mathematics for the best position for the proposed lens in its relation to Earth and sun. Mexone, draft out a message to the Pagans giving them an ultimatum, for General Milford to read to them over the radio. Thania, find out from the guard where we can obtain an accurate map of the world. I want to know where the major Pagan cities are— We've got to work faster than we've ever done before."

And this was exactly what the Crusaders did. General Milford, at the close of issuing a reply to the Pagans and a promise to hand over the five by midnight found himself struck, metaphorically, by a whirlwind. Orders came so thick and fast that he had a hard job to keep track of them, willing though he was to comply with every detail. The well-equipped laboratories were commandeered, the armies of scientists, all experts in their different fields, paced at the disposal of the five Crusaders; and in various directions throughout the Normals' hemisphere things were ordered, worked upon, and brought to fruition. Conscious of the shortness of time, the Amazon never let up the pressure, hardly even pausing to eat. In charge of operations, with the consent of the others, her orders were promptly obeyed, difficult though they were in some cases.

And towards 9 o'clock that evening, following Herculean effort, there were distinct signs of work having been done exactly as required. The laboratories had converted various machines to Abna and the Amazon's specifications and made of them duplicating equipment, with which, during the late afternoon, patterns were made of all five Crusaders—perfect flesh-and-blood images needing only chemicals and electronics to bring the hearts into action and fill the lungs with the breath of life.

Once this was done, towards 10 o'clock, the Amazon and Abna recorded their orders on a vibratory amplifier and then transferred the orders into the dormant but receptive brains of the duplicates, so that they would know exactly what to do. At the end of this particular effort the Amazon and Abna were quite satisfied that the five 'carbon copies' would do exactly as required of them whatever the external conditions. The robots had every detail, even to the mathematics that Viona had worked out with the help of Normal scientists and computers.

The last two hours the Amazon spent with General Milford, explaining the setup to him, putting him in complete charge, and handing over to him the ultimatum to the Pagans, which Mexone had drafted out. Though Milford had only a natural man's grasp of the situation he responded as manfully as he could to the super-scientific, rapid-fire explanations, which the Amazon gave him. When finally she had finished he sat staring at her, surprised that despite the hurricane of mental and physical energy she had passed through she did not look in the least tired.

"There you have the main details," she said. "The rest will take a little time, of course, but I leave it to you to act with all speed. A spaceship will take the duplicates to Mercury, and they will take with them the necessary machine tools to construct a lens. Amongst those papers I have given you, you will find every detail of the machines needed for the construction of the lens, while the necessary optics are already impressed in the minds of the duplicates themselves. From what I have seen of your laboratories the machine tools will not be difficult to manufacture. The other scientific details like the angling of the lens into position and so forth is not your concern: The duplicates will do all that from the knowledge in their brains. Once the duplicates have been launched to Mercury they will handle things for themselves, but you must see to it that they have full control of their spaceship in order to give it a safe landing."

"I will personally supervise that point," Milford promised. "There is only one other thing— How and when do I issue the ultimatum?"

The Amazon shrugged. "Whenever you wish once we are in the hands of the Pagans. Let the threat be with them constantly. Once you have done that leave nothing unturned to dispatch the duplicates to Mercury as quickly as possible. They themselves have enough reasoning power, mechanical though it may be, to know how to defend the lens if it is attacked, and they will not put the lens into position for striking the Earth unless you issue the single radio command— *'Strike!'* That word, received in their built-in radio ears, which require no receiver, will be enough to start them on the final stage of the plan, which I pray will never happen. If in the end they have to carry things through, the impressions recorded on their brains will show them which Pagan cities to incinerate."

"I understand," Milford acknowledged quietly; then for a long moment he looked into the Amazon's violet eyes. "And you? And those who work so loyally with you? What do you intend doing?"

"That I cannot say until we are actually in the situation. My main object—the object of us all in fact—will be to fight for time to give you, the scientists, and the duplicates the chance to turn round. We know what we are getting into, but somehow—there was a faraway look in the Amazon's eyes—"I feel we'll come through."

Milford rose and held out his hand. "You know we will do our part as far as we can. Unfortunately, we don't possess the superhuman qualities of you and your colleagues. We shall pray for the day when you come back to us, your mission accomplished."

The Amazon smiled, shook the hand held out to her, and then characteristically, said no more. She returned to her own quarters where the others were waiting. They said no word but looked at her expectantly.

"It's all arranged?" Abna asked quietly.

"Everything. All we can do is gain as much time as possible and hope for the best." The Amazon glanced at her watch. "It is forty five minutes to midnight. We had better summon the guard of truce and then be on our way.

I take it that we are all ready?"

"Completely," Viona answered promptly. "It will take more than a bunch of Pagans to finish us."

The Amazon smiled a little at Viona's contempt for danger, which was so typical of her. Even Mexone, who rarely said much, was clearly grimly ready for whatever might happen—but with Thania it was different. The newest recruit to the Crusaders' ranks was manifestly nervous, even though she tried with teenage bravado not to show it. Thania smiled rather shakily as the Amazon put an arm round her shoulders. It was one of those moments when affection, never a very strong point with the Golden Amazon, made itself evident through the cold science and matter-of-fact manner.

"You're making a brave show of hiding your feelings, Thania," the Amazon murmured. "But you can't fool me, you know. Naturally, you are apprehensive—we all are, but we have strength and intelligence on our side; and also something that the Pagans haven't got nor ever will have unless they mend their ways. Stated simply, we have Right on our side, and that has always sustained us through every difficulty. Okay?" The soft yet vibrantly muscular arm tightened for a moment around the slim youngster's shoulders.

"Okay," Thania muttered. "I never expected a joyride anyhow when I joined the Crusaders. Whatever you others can do, I can."

"I'll call the guard," Abna said, who had been watching the little scene in silence. "Sooner we get started now, the better."

He turned and moved with majestic tread towards the door.

CHAPTER 6

Plan for Death

It was exactly midnight when the five Crusaders, accompanied by a guard from Lanatock—all of them with white truce badges on their uniforms—entered the Ruling Headquarters of Railstrom. In a few minutes they had passed down Roman-style corridors to a vast chamber of pillars that reminded them of the biggest ballroom they had ever seen. Here, everything was tiled, and the floor was a miracle of mosaic art. The pillars, for their part, supported the up-thrusting cupola of roof, itself a masterpiece of the stonemason's artistry. Plainly, the architecture of ancient Rome was being adhered to throughout.

The final touch came when a figure in a cardinal-red robe emerged from the wilderness of stonework at the back of the colossal place and advanced with regal tread. The Crusaders watched his progress narrowly, and as he came nearer his features became more clearly revealed.

They were thin, almost emaciated, with a high bald forehead and piercing light gray eyes. His temperament seemed somehow to be instantly revealed by the vicious downward curve of the thin-lipped mouth. A man of few sentiments, the Amazon decided, and probably one who believed in cruelty for cruelty's sake.

"Greetings, Crusaders," he acknowledged finally, as he came up to them. "It is gratifying to know that you appreciate the serious nature of my ultimatum..." A cold smile broke the set hardness of his face. "My name is Karg, and my position is that of leader of the Pagans. Normally I am domiciled in our capital city on the old site of London, but for present purposes it seems expedient that I should be here."

"There is hardly a need for you to be sociable in your approach," the Amazon answered curtly. "You demanded our presence, and we are here It is to be hoped that you will honor your part of the bargain and withhold from attacking five unnamed towns."

"But of course..." The frigid eyes expressed vague surprise. "Everything is exactly as it should be, with your own unwarrantable interference under control! Because you are a woman of Earth Amazon, I can speak to you freely. You know the kind of Government that used to exist, and the constant friction that arose because of it. That was changed long ago by my predecessors and myself, and in time the parts of the world that held out against us were brought under control. The old order has gone and a new one is sweeping the Earth. The doctrine of power—the inflexible determination to crush all that that does not conform to the standards we have set... In the name of Balibus, it is so."

"Balibus? The idol?" the Amazon hazarded.

"Exactly so. The symbol in which we believe, and in which the whole world must finally believe. Balibus is emblematic of power, of domination, of progress—disavowed from the sentiments of an earlier time. I repeat, Balibus is a symbol of our power: it is not an idol. We have outgrown the foolishness of worshipping an image. We do not worship anything but Power, which Balibus typifies. So," Karg finished, shrugging, "you will appreciate, I feel, that your own way of life does not match up with the standard on Earth today. That is why I must dispose of you. There is no personal animosity in it; in fact we admire your scientific skill. But it is dangerous to us—so dangerous that the perpetrators of it must be destroyed. You have only General Milford to thank for your present position. He should not have been so foolish as to bring you back to Earth where you are not wanted."

"On the contrary," the Amazon retorted, "it would seem that he did it only just in time! Incidentally, Karg, you will know from the records how an attempt was made to dominate the world in the late 1930's. Those would-be conquerors also had a symbol. I do not think I need to remind you what happened to it... I have particular reason to remember that period for I was born amidst the carnage and was made what I am with the intended purpose of leading those who could break the oppressors. That did not become necessary—but perhaps I have been called to do it in a later age."

Again Karg smiled icily. "I think not, Golden Amazon. My plans for you, and those with you, are complete. Later, when none of you are no longer with us, I shall take over that excellent spaceship you were forced to leave: it can aid us in our reaching outward to the stars. I have little doubt but what our instruments can trace its whereabouts."

"Perhaps," the Amazon answered enigmatically, and Karg seemed as though he were trying to read something from her unfathomable eyes. Then Mexone broke the tension with a curt question.

"Well, what are we waiting for? What do you plan to do?"

Karg shrugged. "It is all arranged. I and the Council

have decided. You are all much too important to pass away unnoticed—so we are agreed that your annihilation shall come in the arena. Perhaps," Karg finished reflectively, "it will serve as an object lesson to those amongst us who have ideas of—er—disloyalty. Tomorrow the general populace will attend in the public arena here. That order has already gone forth."

The Amazon said: "I am prompted to comment upon the curious similarity between Railstrom's methods and the barbarities of ancient Rome. I have usually found that the evolution of intelligence produces a less primitive outlook—so I confess that in respect to you and your people you do not seem to have progressed very much."

Karg said dryly: "I am grieved indeed that there is something that the omniscient Amazon does not understand. I would have said that that is impossible. However, perhaps I ought to explain that we have found the refinements of science are not always effective where our people are concerned. They learn more—objectively—from the terrors of the wild animal arena than from any scientific lethal weapon, hence the public executions of men and women at the hands of wild beasts. We do of course use an electrified lethal chamber in many cases, but the excitement and battle of the arena is never to be deplored... In another respect, however, we do make concession to science."

"How?" Abna asked, in the silence.

"We get rid of the dead much more effectually than do the Normals. We do not rely on burial or cremation. We have a method of complete elimination that leaves not a single bone."

It seemed that for a moment there was a gleam in the Amazon's eyes.

"Very efficient indeed," she commented. "What do you do?"

Karg gave his thin smile. "To such as you, with your immense scientific knowledge, there will be nothing magical about it, hut it certainly looks that way to the uninitiated fools who make up most of our population—which in turn helps to build up the legend of mystical power around me and my fellows." Karg mused for a moment and then asked a question: "You are aware, I take it, of the prevalence of natural radium mines in this part of southern England?"

"I certainly am aware of them," the Amazon replied, as the others—not as informed about England as she was—remained silent. "I know that many generations ago, before this present era, southern England was a mass of pitchblende and uranium, and other radioactive elements."

"Exactly so, mines which today are pure radium, as well as something else," Karg said. "The main radiations given off in the depths of these mines are from radium, but there are magnetic and disintegrative radiations as well... To cut a long story short, dead bodies thrown into these mines disintegrate fairly swiftly and finally vanish forever. The populace—specially insulated of course—is allowed to view these areas from special galleries in the underground workings, but they never find these bodies even though they know they were thrown into the depths. We claim it is magical power which makes the bodies vanish—to further enhance our prestige, you understand—but I am telling you the real scientific trick. It cannot matter if I do since you will not be alive long enough to pass the secret on."

"You seem very confident," the Amazon remarked, with a cold little smile.

"I have reason to be, Amazon... However, we have talked enough and we are wasting time, a thing that I abhor. Tomorrow you will understand." Karg turned and pressed a button. "I hope you will find your quarters—temporary, alas!—completely comfortable."

The Amazon was about to reply then she checked herself as the guard entered. He saluted and looked at Karg expectantly.

"You know what to do," Karg said, then he stood impassively watching as the five had their weapons stripped from them. Only then did he speak again:

"It has been an honor to meet you, my friends. So regrettable that our acquaintance has to be brief..."

* * * *

The quarters of which Karg had spoken proved to he anything but comfortable. They comprised two prison cells connected by a barred door, which at the moment was left open so the five could wander from one cell to the other as they wished. The reason for this was plainly that one cell alone would not have been big enough for all of them... Not that the advantage did them any good: they were prisoners just the same with a guard pacing relentlessly up and down the corridor outside, once the main cell door had been slammed and locked. Only when this had happened did the five take stock of the situation, the yellow ceiling light casting down on their grim faces.

"Well, what now?" Mexone demanded, sitting on the edge of one of the bunks. "We've walked completely into it, Amazon. I hope you realize it."

"Of course I realize it, and you know exactly why I did it..." The Amazon was lounging in the doorway, which connected with the second cell. "Probably we could get out of here if we chose, but since we'd never get clear of the city itself it would be a waste of time… Besides, we don't want to be around loose. Better to be believed dead and give our duplicates a chance to work in peace. Naturally, all the heat will be taken off us once we're believed dead."

"All of which adds up to what?" Viona questioned. "We're *not* dead yet, even though I suspect we soon shall be once we're turned loose in that arena tomorrow."

"Frankly," Mexone commented, "I don't see how we get out of this no matter what we do."

The Amazon came forward into the center of the cell. In the dim light she seemed to be smiling faintly. She said:

"Up to now we've laid no plans because we didn't know what we would be getting into… Right?"

"Right." Viona agreed. "So?"

"So I think we have found the answer—and it was Karg himself who gave it to us, all unwittingly. When he was talking about using the radium mines for disposing of dead bodies from the arena."

"But how—" Mexone started to say; then he was waved into silence.

"Our line of escape," the Amazon said quietly, "lies in—death."

As she saw the astounded faces turned to her she continued: "Up to now, in all our adventures, we have faced it often enough without ever really experiencing it. This time we may have to gamble with it to secure our ends."

"I don't like the sound of that at all," Thania said nervously, and the Amazon glanced towards her.

"I hardly expected you to—but hear me out. I know the mines of which Karg speaks—or at least I did do many generations ago, and they are genuine radium deposits. In the interval of time since the old days the radiations given off have obviously increased in potency, which may be the key to our problem."

"Meaning?" Abna asked quietly.

"Meaning that our lives, in actuality, passed out long ago. We are all of us living on what we might call borrowed power—enormous strength and power produced by laboratory wizardry. The point is that this artificial stimuli we all live with can be restored to its original strength, if ever destroyed, by the emanation of radium radiations. They would destroy an ordinary dead body, as Karg pointed out, but we wouldn't suffer that fate. Provided there is no destruction of vital organs, such as heart, lungs, and so forth, we would return to life very quickly in radium radiation, even though being pronounced dead before this happened. And, fortunately, Karg does not know of this possibility."

"I begin to see what you mean," Abna breathed. "If we meet death in the arena our bodies will be consigned to the radium mines and then come to life again!"

"Exactly," the Amazon acknowledged. "And the advantage is that we shall be seen to be dead before thousands of spectators. There will be no doubt about it. And when our bodies are found to have disappeared from the mines the conclusion will be that the radiations have destroyed us completely."

"It's a marvelous idea," Viona muttered. "Typical of you, mother. The only hard part will be facing death… Yet will it *be* so hard for people like ns? Perhaps it won't seem like anything more than going to sleep."

"Whatever the experience of death may be we have to endure it," the Amazon said, "because it is the logical way out. And then…" Her violet eyes gleamed. "And then, once we have returned to life retribution will really descend on Karg. Those who have presumably died will return to harry and hound him until his vile empire crashes round his ears."

There was a long silence as the enormity and daring of the plan were digested. Then finally it was Thania who spoke:

"I'm ready to try it, whatever the risk, because I have absolute faith in you, Amazon. But I would point out one possibility as I see it."

The Amazon looked at her. "Yes? I'm listening."

"Well you have said that we'll return to life so long as no vital organs are destroyed—but in the arena out there we may be called upon to fight wild animals which will tear us limb from limb. It death comes in that way, how are we ever to revive?

"That's a point," Abna admitted dubiously.

"And one I have considered," the Amazon said. "If we vanquish the wild animals, as we probably shall, Karg will seek to destroy us even then. We shall ask—or I shall—that we may die as real Crusaders in one of the lethal chambers they use—or so Karg himself told us. We shall have to watch our opportunity as far as that is concerned."

"Usually," Abna remarked dryly, "our main concern is to watch how to save our lives, but this time we want to find the most convincing way of losing them! Let it never be said that we don't have variety."

"And if it doesn't work?" Mexone asked soberly. "If we meet death and the radium vibrations don't revive us, what then?"

"Then it is the end," the Amazon responded, with complete acceptance of the horrible alternative.

"If we really do die in the finish, the story as far as

we are concerned is told… But we are not going to," she finished grimly. "We were brought back to Earth to fulfill a mission, and fulfill it we shall The best thing we can do now is get some sleep, and then we'll see what tomorrow brings."

* * * *

Completely decided in her own mind what she was going to do, the Amazon slept soundly enough, and so in a more fitful kind of way—Thania in particular—did the others. When they awakened again the summer sun was just rising and a rough breakfast was being thrust through the metal square in the cell door. Quietly and soberly, each busy with his or her thoughts, the five ate and drank and exchanged few words. They knew what was ahead of them, and it was definitely a situation beyond comment.

After perhaps half an hour, and the meager 'breakfast' finished, a guard entered. Behind him came the scarlet-clad Karg his snakelike eyes darting from one to the other of the Crusaders as though he suspected some kind of a trick. He smiled cynically, as he beheld their subdued expressions.

"With regret," he said, "I have to inform you that the moment has come for you to enter the arena. Before you do so I would be glad of a few final words with you."

"Why?" the Amazon asked, uncompromisingly. "There is nothing more to be said, is there? As for your regret a moment ago, don't be such a hypocrite, Karg. You've only beaten us because we elected to walk into your clutches. Otherwise you would have had us to reckon with!"

"And will continue to do so for longer than you perhaps think," Abna added enigmatically.

Karg hesitated for a moment, obviously unsure of what he was up against. Then evidently his thoughts finally resolved into a pattern for he gave his humorless smile.

"We are wasting time," he said. "Out with them!"

He made a brief signal to the guard and the five submitted to being led from the cell, down the long corridor of the prison, and so out into the fresh morning air. From the prison a closed van conveyed them to the arena. This they could only guess at since the van had no windows… But the moment the vehicle stopped and they stepped outside they realized that their guess had been correct. The van had entered the arena itself, and this time the rows of seats overlooking the big amphitheatre were filled with men and women in a fervor of excitement.

Saying nothing but remaining close together the five watched the van recede, pass through the same gateway they had once scaled to steal an airplane—then they were alone, and yet not alone. The mood of thousands of spectators was plain from the character of their cries. Either they were putting on an act to please their ruler or else they were genuinely governed by an avid desire to see battle commence.

"Do you suppose," Mexone asked, "that even now we could drive some kind of bargain with Karg for a quick death which would leave our bodies intact?"

"Hardly," Abna replied grimly. "With all these spectators he will have to put on a show, with us as the principal actors, unfortunately. No; I'm afraid we'll have to go through with it."

He put his mighty arm round the shoulders of Thania and smiled at her encouragingly. She said nothing, but he could feel her trembling against him. For a moment, rage against Karg overwhelmed his habitual calm—then again he was master of himself. Beside him, the Amazon, Viona, and Mexone stood tensely wondering how much longer the tension was likely to last… The noise from the assembled populace grew louder—disquieting, angry, vicious—then it abated suddenly before a voice from a loudspeaker, the very same one which once before had spoken to the Crusaders.

It was the voice of Karg himself, hidden somewhere where he could come to no harm.

"People of Railstrom! Today you behold before you in the arena not five who have proven disloyal to us but five who have tried to undermine our very existence. Five who thought they could uproot and destroy the Pagans—five who lay claim to super-scientific powers and mastery of the cosmos itself. You have heard of the Cosmic Crusaders? Well, there you behold them! Such must always be the fate of those who try to cross swords with us, the invincible Pagans…"

Suddenly, shatteringly, there was a vast roar of approval. It died as Karg's voice came forth again, his words booming like thunder across the arena.

"Today, citizens of Railstrom, you will have a feast of sport indeed. Our supposedly superhuman friends will fight—and die. We shall soon see if physique and mentality can overcome the beasts now launched upon them!"

Again the thunderous roar from the crowd. The Amazon glanced about the arena, and finally her eyes settled on a grilled gate being slowly raised, the same gate indeed that had been opened on their previous excursion into the amphitheater. The crowd became quiet, watching and waiting tensely.

"It won't be long now," Mexone murmured, clenching his fists. "We can soon—Good heavens!" he broke off. "Look!"

The Amazon, Viona, Abna, and Thania were already

doing so, steeling their nerves and muscles to the sight of five huge bull-gorillas waddling into the arena. Each of them was possibly close to eight feet tall and plainly the most savage of their species.

"We don't stand a chance against those!" Thania gasped.

"We're not supposed to," the Amazon retorted, separating herself from the others and standing ready for action. "Karg wants us killed, don't forget, and brutes like this can tear us in pieces if we aren't careful." She watched the shaggy anthropoids as their red-flecked eyes darted hungrily about the arena. "All I can say is—do the best you can."

Suddenly the tension was broken as the monsters charged, bellowing with tremendous rage. The spectators roared their approval. This was decidedly something new—super beings against gorillas and there didn't seem the least doubt that the gorillas would win—and quickly.

But it wasn't quite so simple as that. The gorillas most certainly charged, but when they arrived at the spot where the five should have been they found they had vanished. Each one had waited until the last second and then leapt with enormous force info the air, carrying themselves over the heads of their aggressors. They landed, twisted round, and made ready for the next charge.

"We can never defeat monsters like this without weapons," the Amazon panted, her eyes never leaving the enraged anthropoids as they prepared to attack again. "There's only one way out—we must try and hypnotize them. You hear that?" she demanded of the others.

"The idea's all right if Thania doesn't go to pieces like she did the last time," Viona responded, rather brutally—but Thania did not have much chance to notice what Viona had said for the brutes charged again.

And this time the battle was really on. All five found themselves in the clutch of a beast apiece, fighting for their lives against the merciless steel-strong hands and snapping jaws. The Amazon's idea of hypnosis was simply unworkable and the five were thrown back on the only resource they had—physical strength. Death they wanted, certainly, but not this way, and that realization released in them all the muscled retaliation and fury of which they were capable. Even from Thania, who faced with this situation found her last trace of fear vanishing before the rage that consumed her.

The spectators were certainly treated to something they had not expected. The five human figures, small beside those of the gorillas, dodged this way and that in the arena, or were engaged in the midst of tearing struggle in which more-than-human muscles were pitted against the sheer brute strength of the subhuman beasts.

The Amazon in particular was in the midst of a life-and-death struggle. She had not succeeded in dodging as the others had done, with the result that she was in the grip of one of the brutes, his snapping jaws striving to reach her throat and tear out her jugular vein. Desperately aware of this endeavor, she locked her fingers in the short neck of the attacking anthropoid and crushed—and crushed, her legs clamped round his waist and every ounce of her vast strength thrown into the effort.

As she fought on against the snarling jaws and yellow fangs, she caught a glimpse of the others—of Abna delivering sledge-hammer punches into the stomach of the brute attacking him; of Viona leaping nimbly and trying, with some success, to break one of the other gorilla's arms with a ju-jitsu hold; of Mexone kicking, leaping and punching and somehow escaping the vicing arms—and lastly Thania, endeavoring by the sheer strangling power of her fingers to keep the snapping fangs of her attacker away from her throat.

Gasping, surrounded by earth-shaking din, the Amazon had to concentrate on her own troubles again as she was thrown to the ground. A savage hand lashed at her and tore her costume from throat to waist—a rip that certainly would have gouged open her chest had it been a fraction closer.

Half stunned, she lay for a moment watching for her chance. She wriggled out of the way of the plunging feet, flinging out both hands towards one of the gorilla's ankles as he plunged downwards towards her with a bellow of frustrated rage.

Throwing everything into a last effort she pulled mightily on the hairy leg and her eyes glinted in triumph as, caught off balance, the gorilla found one foot flying from under him. He came down on his face with earth-shaking concussion, and almost instantly the Amazon was on his back, her knees nipping tightly into his body and her supple forearms round his throat.

The others did not see what had happened: they were too busy fighting for themselves, but the spectators did and they marveled. They marveled at this slim, satiny yellow being who gradually got her knees into the small of the gorilla's back and then pulled with her rounded arms until the brute was in a hopeless position with his bull neck forced back to an unnatural angle by the vice-like grip under his chin.

Back and forth the Amazon pitched as the creature struggled, but she never once let go her grip. In fact she tightened it with every moment, her eyes tightly shut and her teeth clenched in a snarl of vast energy. Tendons and muscles bulged under her golden skin where her costume had been ripped away—until suddenly it was over. The massive neck broke with a crack like a pistol shot. The anthropoid fell heavily forward, pitching the Amazon from his dead body. She lay for a few seconds with dust flying in her face and blood streaming from the cuts and scratches she had received... Moments passed until the fury of the battle going on around her roused her to one elbow as she surveyed the scene.

A second gorilla lay dead near Abna, and he was in the midst of subjecting another one to grueling punishment—mainly a hail of violent blows to the stomach, all of them delivered with the awful power of his steel muscles. There came an end to it finally: the breath blasted out of him the gorilla could take no more and it succumbed to unconsciousness as a mighty blow, and a lucky one, struck it on the point of the jaw. It went down with a crash, not dead but certainly knocked out.

Which left only two of the brutes to deal with, and massive and savage though they were they were already taking plenty of punishment from Mexone, Viona, and Thania, all of them unleashed to the limit of their strength and fury, and looking decidedly the worse for wear in the process.

It seemed as though even the gorillas' tiny brains had at last registered the fact that here was something they could not handle. The strength and agility of their adversaries was something they had never bargained for.

The Amazon, as she struggled to her feet, caught Abna's eye and she gave a grim smile and a nod. At that they both hurled themselves forward together and joined in the battle with the remaining brutes. The addition of two more superhumanly strong beings to add to the misery of the wrenching and pummeling they were already receiving was too much for the last two gorillas. They turned and fled, snarling in pain and fury, towards the gateway from which they had originally emerged…

CHAPTER 7

Back from the Dead

The five straightened slowly as they watched their foes go. They looked at each other significantly as the brutes finally vanished through the gateway, the gate itself dropping down behind them; then the Amazon turned to the matter of her various wounds and the tears in her costume. She, and the others likewise, were in the midst of ministering to themselves when a sudden roar from the gathered spectators, made them glance up. It seemed somehow that it was a roar of approval, probably for what they had done—then their gaze settled on Karg's scarlet-garbed figure standing on a rostrum to the forefront of the gathered spectators. He seemed small due to his distance away, but his voice boomed forth through the microphone in front of him.

"You are to be congratulated, Crusaders, upon a valiant fight, but let it be understood that that does not imply your freedom. You are convicted and must pay the penalty of death That you haven't done so at the hands of the gorillas is entirely due to your phenomenal strength—and to our way of thinking you would again triumph over whatever beasts we loosed upon you."

There was a murmuring amongst the people, and it sounded very much as though they were displeased with the ruler's words. Perhaps, even, they did not agree that the Crusaders should remain condemned after the way they had acquitted themselves. But, all powerful, Karg went on talking and stilled the murmuring with upraised arms.

"Crusaders, I command that you come here! Immediately!"

For a moment the Amazon hesitated, then she looked at the others and gave a shrug.

"Better do as he says," she advised. "This may be what we're looking for. Come on."

She started moving across the arena, adjusting the rips in her tights as she went. The others did likewise and followed behind her until at length they were immediately in front of and below the rostrum, looking up at Karg several feet above them. Around him, seated, were the various grim-faced members of his retinue.

"I have to admit to your strength," he said finally, "and as I have said it is a thousand pities that vanquishing of the beasts in the arena does not earn you your freedom. That perhaps might have been possible were you not the Cosmic Crusaders. As the situation stands, you have merely side-stepped one fate and earned for yourselves another."

Again the angry murmuring of the people. Karg ignored it and continued:

"For what you have done, and for what you are, there can only be one answer—death. Not at the hands of beasts again, but in a manner which you will appreciate. Scientific death, painless and instantaneous."

The Amazon smiled faintly and said nothing. Karg considered her, plainly a little puzzled.

"You smile?" he questioned, faintly irritated. Is the prospect of death so amusing?"

"One can smile at one's thought," the Amazon replied

enigmatically. Then her tone became grim. "Of one thing I would warn you, Karg. Our death will not mean our extinction or the end of our crusade and ideals. For you, woe will begin when we die."

There was silence for a moment as Karg's cold eyes measured the Amazon's violet ones over the intervening distance. He for his part vaguely wondered if he regretted destroying this extraordinary beautiful woman; while she for her part was regretting that her words had not carried to the spectators in general, an impossibility without the aid of a microphone... Then the noise of the spectators began to rise again a swelling roar, until finally Karg turned impatiently.

"Silence—or I will have the arena cleared!" He motioned to a waiting group of distant guards and then continued, "So be it, Crusaders. There is no room on this planet for both of us with our ideas so diametrically opposed. You must consider this the end of your scientific reign. All of you will meet scientific death, as I have already said, and after that your bodies will be consigned to the radioactive mines, the mausoleum of all those who believe their ideals are superior to ours."

The five said nothing. Indeed there was nothing they *could* say. They stood watching in cold defiance as the guards came up...

* * * *

At precisely 6 o'clock that evening the five silent Crusaders in the midst of a heavy guard were escorted to the death chamber—a place of metal with enormous electrodes spearing from the walls, presumably connected with an electric supply. The guards withdrew, the metal door was clamped from the outside, and the five were alone, literally facing death with no way out.

"So we take the final gamble," the Amazon said quietly, her arm going about Thania's shoulders. "If it succeeds, Karg's power will certainly be broken. If it does not..." She hunched one shoulder for a moment. "There is no sense in dwelling on that. We mustn't. To return to Earth to be beaten by a power-mad idiot like Karg would be ignominy indeed."

She said no more, becoming suddenly conscious, as were the others, of the electric current creeping upon them. Thania quivered for a moment, the Amazon gave her an encouraging smile and then held out her right hand to Abna. He took it gently, his left arm around Viona's waist.

So they waited, and with the seconds the current intensified—and intensified yet again, until what had begun with a tingling of the limbs was now a complete numbness and they could feel their senses drifting into an enormous gulf—a gulf ever greater that ended in utter darkness...

* * * *

And through days, weeks, months the darkness persisted for the Crusaders—the darkness of the Unknown in which nothing was, in which they died and were removed without ceremony to the depths of the radium mines, there to be left to the disintegrative power of the radiations about them. And whilst all this was taking place, five expressionless, unemotional duplicates were at work, transported to little Mercury in the fastest time possible.

Their departure attracted no attention from the all-powerful Pagans, but their movements were watched attentively by the Normals through the medium of powerful telescopes. The instruments were not strong enough to show what was happening on the surface of Mercury: the main idea was to catch a glimpse of a lens in space, which would reveal when the interplanetary engineering work was done.

And once on the hell planet, the impregnated brains of the robots went to work and their basically mechanical bodies obeyed all the orders given them. They worked in spacesuits on the airless exterior of the planet—since it was essential they should continue to draw breath and keep their lungs working—but this was the only concession they needed. Otherwise, they worked for 24 Earth-hours at a stretch, oblivious to the furnace heat of Mercury's dayside, undazzled by the white hot glare of sunlight on the arid, chasm-split plains. They worked with a purpose, with the swift, mechanical sureness of machines. They toiled on the edges of molten metal lakes: They walked endless miles with heavy crucibles; they fashioned a vast circle of glass from raw molten elements and, in the light gravity, finally succeeded in carrying it in perfectly aligned sections to the night side of the planet where the glass cooled to brittle hardness after being first exposed to the varying-temperature of hot and cold in sunlight and shadow.

Under the icy stars the robots toiled on, amidst a rocky plain that was sundered by a terrible frost, until at last the job was done… Then came the next stage—the need to transfer the engineering masterpiece into the depths of space. This too they accomplished, as a fresh sequence of orders in their mechanical brains took over.

They snared the mighty lens, occupying when assembled in full a diameter nearly all of the size of Mercury when assembled in full, and transported the sections into space by the use of attractors on their spaceship. The various pieces were taken to a point in the void where the gravity of the Sun, Mercury, and to a lesser extent Venus, held them in place, equi-balanced and ready for assembly.

From then on the robots worked with the same tireless energy, but in space this time—joining the sections together with flawless precision and bonding the joints with machines specially created for the task… And the mighty lens grew, in a place prescribed by Viona and the mathematical machines specially created for the task…a tiny gleaming star when seen from Earth, angled in such a way that, as yet, no solar rays were concentrated through it—but it was ready nonetheless for moving into position—a simple job in free space—the moment the need arose.

And as these tireless, sexless engineers worked to the final stages there came an awakening to the five buried deep in the mausoleum of the radium mines—a slow reintegration of intelligence and movement as the radiations of radium and a dozen other radioactive elements, continued to work ceaselessly upon them.

The Amazon became aware of consciousness first, and Abna shortly afterwards. It was akin to awakening from a deep sleep. They fastened their eyes on a faintly luminous dark, and wondered—and thought—until at last the tides of memory began to return, and with it the realization—for the Amazon at least—that the gamble with death had succeeded. Then, by degrees, Thania, Mexone and Viona also recovered and the five were able to converse and discuss the marvel of science that had taken place.

"Well, we're alive again," Abna said, with sober satisfaction. "And we owe that fact to you. Vi. Your judgment was right."

"Yes, thank heaven," she agreed quietly. "Our clothes feel pretty well rotted, but that's about the only inconvenience. The next thing we've got to do is get out of here and find out how long a time has passed, and exactly what is going on. After that we need food, fresh clothes, and then we'll attend to friend Karg—and is he going to be surprised!"

Escape from the mines presented no difficulty since, being a mausoleum open to the public curiosity, it had galleries and stairways leading to the surface. So the five emerged eventually into the evening light and surveyed. Then they looked at each other—ragged, their black tights falling to pieces.

"Everything looks just the same," the Amazon said, making herself as decent as her garments permitted. "We can assume, I think, that no burning lens has gone into action." She glanced at the cloudy evening sky. "From the feel of things it is summer—and it will also be night soon—then we can move. Until then we had perhaps better stay here."

This they decided upon, but as soon as night came they were on the move, traveling with swift silence through the darkness toward the small landing field, which lay back of the arena. To cover the distance from the mines to the arena they 'borrowed' a fast car and eventually reaching the high wall around the enclosure they searched for and then climbed over one of the many small gates erected for entrance and exit… And it was a journey worth making for there were several planes standing deserted on the landing field.

"Good," the Amazon murmured, her eyes gleaming. "Our first move must be to General Milford and let him know of our escape. Then—some food, a brief rest and repair these clothes. And afterwards…" She smiled coldly. "Well, we'll see. Let's go. Now seems to be as good a time as any."

Such it proved to be, with the darkness covering all

their movements. In any case, since they were supposed to be dead, there was no special alert in operation to watch for them. There were one or two uniformed men drifting about the edges of the plane field but they gave no trouble—or even noticed the ill-clothed interlopers in the darkness—and so the nearest plane was gained and Abna thankfully shut the control cabin door. It took the Amazon perhaps ten minutes to figure out the workings of the plane's control board, then satisfied that the gauge showed plenty of fuel aboard she started up the motors and fled into the cloudy, drizzly sky. The others, grouped about the windows, smiled as they watched the queer little airstrip falling away below them...

When the five Crusaders presented themselves in General Milford's headquarters toward one in the morning, he—though warned in advance by radio of their coming—was completely taken aback. Then he shook hands with them warmly.

"My friends—my very dear friends, you escaped! I couldn't really believe it even though you radioed to me. The news from the Pagans has said so distinctly that you died long ago."

"We died all right," the Amazon agreed, "but due to certain radioactivity, of which I'll tell you in a less strained moment, we recovered life again, and came here immediately. Karg does not know what has happened to us. He thinks our bodies have disintegrated by radiation. He'll discover his mistake in time."

Milford nodded urgently. "Yes, yes, of course. Do sit down, my friends—you must be tired. You require refreshments?"

"As soon as possible, along with clothes," the Amazon acknowledged, sitting down. "Then we'll retire to our former headquarters for a while and repair some of the damage sustained to our clothes."

She looked rather ruefully at her torn and hastily repaired tights, then Milford turned to the bell-push and gave the necessary orders to the guard who came in. When he had departed again Milford said, "You know, I presume, how long it is since you died?"

The Amazon shook her head. "Exactly what time has elapsed we don't know. How long has it been?"

"It is nine months and four days since you left here to face what you knew must be certain death."

"That long?" Abna's eyebrows rose in surprise.

"It would probably take that long for the radioactive radiations to revive us," the Amazon said. "Just the same it is a good deal longer than I expected. And it accounts for the lack of surveillance over us too… Well, what has been happening? Have our doubles done their work?"

"Admirably," Milford conceded. "Telescopic observation shows that the space lens is in place in the position desired, but it has not been used as yet… That will come shortly."

"You mean?" the Amazon asked.

"I mean, Amazon, that Karg consistently refused to listen to reason. I issued the ultimatum you drafted, demanding that Karg cease to coerce the Normals, and free from his own territory all those who are not in sympathy with him. He refused point blank, just as he rejected the suggestion that a world plebiscite should be held so the people can decide what kind of government they want—Pagan or Normal. I am quite sure, even as you are, that we would win, but instead of giving the chance Karg has issued a counter ultimatum and ignored my warning of destruction of the Pagans if he does not agree."

"And what is your ultimatum?" the Amazon asked.

"That unless he does as we have asked by midnight tomorrow night certain towns in the Pagan territory will be instantly destroyed. I don't know what the towns are, but since you impressed upon the robots' brains the impressions of where these towns are they will know, and angle the lens accordingly."

"In other words, a declaration of war?" Abna asked grimly.

"I am afraid so. There is no other way. He won't give in, and we do not intend to tolerate his insidious advance any longer. If it comes to war—as apparently it will—there will be severe losses on both sides, but with the lens we shall finally be the winners."

"Probably so," the Amazon mused, "but there will be terrible losses of both innocent and guilty, and that is not our purpose in life. We want this whole thing settled amicably, even if the threat—but not the actual destruction— had to be used. Midnight tomorrow, you say?"

Milford nodded. The Amazon reflected further, then asked, "Have you issued orders to our doubles to strike?"

"I shall do so tonight—to give them time to act."

"I'll do it myself," the Amazon said. "And I'll slightly change the original orders at the same time. I want this business settled without injury if I can—"

The Amazon paused as the guard came in. He saluted and glanced at Milford.

"A meal is waiting in the Crusaders' headquarters," he announced; and then retired again as the General nodded.

"We will refresh and tidy ourselves," the Amazon announced, "then when you are ready to contact the robots inform me and I will do the rest. Since we have come back to the ranks I may as well take control as before. Agreed?"

"Agreed," Milford nodded. "In fact I would much sooner you did since the question now involves such super-scientific forces."

The Amazon smiled, and Milford got to his feet and opened the door in readiness for them.

CHAPTER 8

Karg Escapes

About this time, in his own headquarters in Roman-esque Lexicon, Karg was in the midst of scheming with his immediate associates who comprised the governing body of the Pagans. The schemes were deep and far reaching, involving as they did, early half the Earth and it's population.

"Perhaps," Karg said, during an interval in the discussion, "it is an advantage that Milford has at last thrown down the gauntlet in the way he has. For too long we have been pursuing a policy of persuasion and quiet infiltration. We have always known that war must inevitably result in the final struggle to bring home our message to the world. Violent war, indeed," he shrugged. "But in the end, we, the Pagans, will win. Man prefers to do as he wishes and crush those who cross him, and on the basis of that doctrine there will be few who won't support us... If they don't—" He spread his thin hands expressively.

"You don't think there is any chance of Milford withdrawing his ultimatum?" one of the advisers asked quietly.

"Why should he? He has pronounced himself wearied with our constant coercion of the Normals to our way of living and has threatened us with destruction if we don't cease our activities and release all those who do not wish to follow us. Then he offers a world plebiscite to settle the issue… We can't and won't back down from that. No, my friends, it is the chance we have been waiting for. He's asking for war—and he'll get it."

"And what about his threat to destroy certain towns sometime after midnight tomorrow?"

Karg laughed softly. "Nothing more than a clever attempt at bluff, my friend. Milford speaks rather mysteriously of powers in space, a legacy from the Cosmic Crusaders, but all he is doing is trading on their scientific reputation, There's nothing Milford can do except resort to nuclear weapons—but since we can also do that, and quicker than he can, he is not likely to get very far."

Another asked a question: "In view of Milford's threats, bluff though they may be, might it not be a wise precaution to have space investigated in case he has some secret weapon in the void? The crusaders *might* have left something that he can use—with disastrous results to us."

"Space is already being investigated, from the orbit of Mercury to the asteroids," Karg replied. "I have no fear that we shall be caught unawares… But a weapon in space?" He laughed derisively. "I never heard such nonsense."

He considered for a moment, and then added: "Well, gentlemen, I do not think there is anything more to discuss. We have before us a perfect formula for launching war— and if there is no change by midnight tomorrow night we will launch it with all our power and bring this meddling fool Milford to his knees. Everything is on our side, and thanks once again to Milford's miscalculation in bringing the Crusaders back to Earth we don't even have to worry about them. They are nothing but memories, and somewhere—somewhere—they have a spaceship wandering in the void, which it behoves us to commandeer. We will— once war to establish our rightness is fought and won." Karg made a gesture of finality. "That is all, gentlemen. We will meet again at six tomorrow evening to consider the final details. Good night."

Thus summarily dismissed the advisers rose to their feet, inclined their heads respectfully to the ruler, and then departed. For a long time after they had gone, Karg sat thinking, his lean fingers drumming a mute tune on the arm of his chair. Indeed, near dawn, so lost in thought was he that the sudden buzzing of the radio for attention made him jump. He got to his feet, annoyed at his betrayal of nerves, and crossed to the control panel against the wall. He snapped in the radio control switch.

"Karg speaking. What is your message?"

"Report from Central Radio Interplanetary Station, sir, received from Investigation Space Flight 7."

"Proceed," Karg ordered curtly. "Cut out the preamble details and come right to the point."

"As you command, sir. Space Flight 7 have investigated as ordered, but only one vessel has returned. The rest have been destroyed by some kind of weapon in outer space."

Karg stared fixedly into the spaces of his office. "A weapon in outer space?" he repeated. "What kind of a weapon?"

"Details are not clear from the lone survivor. He reports something like a star in the vicinity of Mercury, which destroyed eleven of the machines investigating. He escaped and I have given you his report."

"His name?" Karg snapped. "I want first hand information from him."

"Commander Quentin Wade, sir—"

"Contact him and have him sent here immediately…"

"Immediately, sir." The radio clicked and Karg switched off. He stood for a moment with his lips compressed and his eyes hard. It took him several seconds to realize that there evidently was a weapon in space after all; and a mighty powerful one if it could destroy eleven tremendously tough spaceships so completely.

"The Crusaders," Karg muttered. "So they did leave a legacy after all. Milford wasn't bluffing."

"No, Karg, he was not bluffing. Nor am I."

The voice was quiet, but it had the ring of steel about it. Karg turned slowly, his hand flying to the weapon in his cardinal-red robe.

"I shouldn't, Karg, if I were you."

He dropped his hand and turned to face the owner of the voice. Though he knew by now to whom it belonged he still could not believe what he saw. The Golden Amazon was only a few feet away, proton gun in her yellow hand, her red-lined cloak flowing from around her black suited figure. Her beautiful face was coldly smiling. Her golden hair was caught back from her high forehead with a glittering diamond clasp.

"It—it isn't possible," Karg whispered. "You died—all of you did. In these past months I have seen you in the mines."

"And now you see me here," the Amazon retorted. "My colleagues are guarding this room, seeing that we are not disturbed. You took on more than you expected when you endeavored to destroy the Cosmic Crusaders! As to how I got in here—Well, you did have the door open for your colleagues to join you in conference, did you not? I came in at that time, having been in the building for some time. I have been behind that tall instrument cabinet, waiting for you, hearing all you had to say."

The Amazon had been moving as she spoke. Now she snatched the gun from Karg's belt, then turned to the radio equipment and switched it on. He turned and watched her in puzzled silence. Finally she spoke again.

"You have been given an ultimatum by General Milford, Karg—one which can put the world at peace and smash forever the domination you seek to impose. I would advise you to accept that ultimatum."

"Your advice is not required," Karg answered curtly, still obviously unsure of himself at finding the Amazon alive. He knew there was trickery somewhere but he could not put his finger on it.

"If you still refuse to comply with Milford's wishes," the Amazon continued as though Karg had never spoken, "the threat of destruction from outer space, already mentioned by him, will become a reality. You are not fighting Milford, Karg—you are fighting *us*!"

Karg did not answer. He merely watched the Amazon with steely eyes.

"Several of your space ships have recently been destroyed," the Amazon continued. "All you know about it is that a brilliant star near Mercury caused the trouble. That star is a giant lens, Karg, as big as Mercury itself, and it was built to my orders by duplicates of myself and my colleagues. It is poised ready now to be turned upon your damnable Pagan cities wherever they may be. I have only to give the word over the radio—" the Amazon tapped the instruments beside her emphatically—"and the robots will obey and strike wherever I order. Refuse Milford's ultimatum and everything you know will vanish in unholy flame. Agree, and you will possibly get away with your life—exiled, and unwanted. That is the choice."

"Bluff does not move me," Karg said at last. "And that

is all I believe your words to be. One who can bluff me into believing you died along with your colleagues will try anything. I refuse to bow to Milford and I do not believe your words."

The Amazon smiled coldly and, still keeping Karg covered, she snapped on the microphone.

"Evidently you require proof, my friend, of what you are up against. From here to Mercury a message takes about six minutes. The robots will hear it because they are designed to do so. It will take them 30 minutes to adjust the lens to the required position I shall outline. Altogether, in less than three quarters of an hour you will have proof. Proof enough, I think, to convince you..."

She became silent, flashing glances at the electric clock on the wall, mentally counting the time until the radio waves should make contact. Finally she spoke again— concisely, her eyes still on Karg.

"Strike on angle 72, intersection 4, allowing for 56 deflection. Strike immediately—then divert until further orders." Silence again.

"What did that mean?" Karg asked at last.

"It was coded instruction which the robots understand. In plain language I told them to angle the space-lens so that its beam strikes directly down on the arena here. They will do it with mathematical precision. The effect will probably do much to change your mind."

Karg clenched his fists, his thin face plainly showing the frustrated fury he was experiencing. His voice trembled with emotion when he spoke again.

"You would deliberately kill to prove your point?"

"Kill? In the arena outside? Hardly."

"A beam spreads out as it goes, Amazon. To pinpoint just the arena, a mere dot on the face of the Earth, is impossible."

"I say it is not, and since I designed the lens I ought to know." The Amazon motioned with her weapon. "I think we should go to the roof of these headquarters of yours and see for ourselves. In less than an hour—and it will take about that time to get action—the sun will be up and you can see for yourself— Move!"

Karg hesitated and glanced towards the door. Evidently not mindful of his own safety he abruptly rushed toward it, but the Amazon's proton gun did not fire as he expected. Instead she stood quietly waiting—with good reason. The moment he yanked the door open, Karg fell back again, staring uncertainly at the massive seven-foot figure of Abna waiting outside. Beyond him again waited Viona, Mexone and Thania, all of them fully armed.

"There's no way out of this, Karg," the Amazon told him calmly, following him up. "Carry on to the roof—and I'll be right behind you."

With so much ranged against him Karg relaxed and smiled bitterly. He began to walk down the passage, and towards the staircase, which led to the roof. The Amazon followed him, her gun ready, but she exchanged a significant look with the others as she passed them.

"We'll keep things safe down here," Abna murmured. "You won't be disturbed."

The Amazon nodded and moved on swiftly. In a moment or two she had caught up with Karg and, perforce, he ascended the spiral stairway that led out on to the roof. He surveyed the gray dawn sky for a moment and then glanced at the Amazon.

"There—to that parapet—" She indicated it with her gun.

Karg eyed her narrowly and obeyed, finishing up at the

parapet and gazing out over the expanse of deserted arena, visible in its entirety from this high elevation.

"I do not imagine we shall have to wait long," the Amazon said. "The sun is up—despite the clouds—which is the major necessity for a solar lens. You will have quite an unforgettable demonstration, Karg."

Karg did not answer. He was too busy searching within his own mind for a way out of the impasse—and he was vaguely confused too since he still could not imagine how the superwoman came to be alive when he had most certainly seen her dead. Reluctantly he began admitting to himself that here was somebody who was more than a match for him.

The minutes passed. There were no sounds in the headquarters building. As yet nobody was astir, and even when they were Abna and the others would see to it that nobody got very far. Karg stirred restlessly but he did not speak. He moved a little and the merciless proton gun followed his every movement.

"Relax, my friend," the Amazon suggested coldly. "You will have your proof soon enough—and once you do maybe I can make you do something sensible." She took a fleeting glance at her watch. "I should say in about another ten minutes."

Karg glared but be did not speak. There was nothing he could do except wait, but he was firmly resolved to take a risk if he saw the slightest opportunity. But the opportunity never came: the Amazon was too alert for that. Then suddenly came that for which she and Karg—perforce—had been waiting. There came a transient and incredible brilliance that was far in excess of daylight. The Amazon and Karg both turned, all else forgotten, their eyes slitted against the brilliance—and though they were only on the edge of the unthinkable effulgence, their eyes were nearly blinded by its intensity.

It lasted perhaps 8 or 10 seconds, generating a warmth that the Amazon and Karg could both feel—but the main core of the concentrated sunlight was upon the arena, a beam which struck through clouds and atmosphere and impinged upon the arena itself, the giant idol, the rows of seats and miscellaneous masonry. All of them instantly began to smoke and generate unbearable heat—and in 10 seconds they were gone, reduced to the molten state and leaving behind a half-mile crater from which acrid smoke rolled in yellow clouds.

The normal daylight returned, seeming to the dazzled eyes of the two watchers to be dull and yellowish-green after the glare they had witnessed.

"You she-devil!" Karg exploded suddenly, all his rage springing ungoverned to the surface. "Only a she-devil would ever conceive a weapon like this—"

He hurled himself forward, regardless of consequences—and because the Amazon was still half blinded from the light, she was not as alert as usual.

Her proton gun went spinning and Karg's fist crashed into her jaw before she knew what had happened. She crashed over on her back and shook her head savagely. Then when she blinked upward through a slowly clearing pink mask across her eyes she saw her own proton gun and Karg's thin hand steadily leveling it.

"Get up," he commanded, himself blinking as he struggled to restore his own eyes to normal.

The Amazon hesitated. Karg made an irritated gesture, thrust a hand under her arm, and jerked her up. She did not attempt resistance for she had reason to know the shattering power of the gun menacing her.

"Now perhaps we can get things on a more equal footing," Karg snapped. "Up to now you have held all the aces, Amazon, but from here on it's going to be a different story." He glanced at the shattered arena and smiled bitterly. "All right, you have convinced me—convinced me that if I hadn't got the better of you a moment ago our cause is lost. It is, however, my method to make use of my defeats."

It was the Amazon's turn to be silent, her mind working fast to devise a way out of this about-turn. But how? Karg was ready for every wrong move, nor was it very likely he had forgotten that Abna, and the others were guarding the passage downstairs.

"I think," Karg said, after a moment, "that this fiendish weapon you have devised, Amazon, should be used after all to give the Pagans the victory, without the silly formality of an ultimatum. I have seen that the robots obey radio orders—you have made that very clear—so I can think of no reason why they should not obey me just as easily."

The Amazon gave a slight start. The fact was that Karg had spoken a truth; the robots would obey any voice and obey orders, unable as they were to discriminate between friend and foe, man or woman.

"That being so," Karg smiled coldly, "you have perhaps given me a mighty victory sooner than you expected, Amazon. Since the robots are already in position for handling and focusing this space lens you speak of, there need be no delay. We will go below—and I will send a message." Karg's tone changed and he added icily, "Move. Back the way we came to the lower regions—and don't imagine I have overlooked the presence of your colleagues down below. The slightest hint of a sign to them and I'll kill you. I only delay now because I need you a while longer. Now move."

The Amazon obeyed, knowing full well there was nothing else she could do. She went slowly down the spiral staircase, Karg immediately behind and above her, his weapon concealed now but nonetheless in readiness. When they reached the floor of the passage he stopped for a moment and roughly twisted the Amazon round to face him.

"Now listen," he said curtly. "My gun—or rather yours—is still here concealed by my tunic, and I will instantly use it on you if I have to. You will tell your friends that I am still in your power and that you have certain plans for me. I will walk beside you, not behind you, in case that makes them suspicious. You understand?"

"Perfectly," the Amazon agreed.

"Very well, then. Proceed."

The Amazon obeyed, striving desperately with every step she took to think of some way out of her difficulty. But there was none. She had completely lost the initiative… So finally she came upon Abna, Thania, Mexone and Viona as they stood near and around Karg's headquarters, still in readiness for whatever might arise.

"Nothing happened yet," Abna announced as they reached the other Crusaders, "beyond a couple of guards who came to report here with a space pilot. Name of Quentin Wade. We dealt with him and the guards: they're tied up in an ante-room when you want them."

"I hardly think I shall," the Amazon said, as Karg gave her a meaning look. "I have plans for Karg here—special plans. The moment I've finished with him I'll be joining you. He is finally convinced that the lens in space is an actuality."

"We saw the flash through the windows," Abna glanced towards them. "I take it the results were satisfactory?"

"Entirely," the Amazon assented. "The arena—and that

godless idol—were both destroyed… Anyway, I must get on. And see that we are not disturbed."

Abna nodded and the Amazon looked him full in the eyes for a moment, trying to exert what telepathic power she had to convey a message. From the expression on Abna's face it was plain that her mental vibrations did not register. He turned away, folded his massive arms, and prepared to wait.

With a sigh the Amazon went forward into Karg's headquarters and he closed the door quietly behind them and snapped over the catch. Then he brought the proton gun into view again.

"You did that quite well," Karg conceded. "Now let us proceed further. You will instruct the robots to turn the lens so it affects Ooberju (Normal City) and destroy it."

"You expect me to issue that order?" the Amazon demanded.

"I do—mainly because you use code words, I believe. You will obviously not name this city since that would mean your own destruction—and if you name any other Pagan city and it is destroyed I shall soon hear of it and deal with you and your colleagues. So—issue the order."

The proton gun waved toward the radio and, her lips tight, the Amazon moved toward the apparatus. Then abruptly Karg checked her.

"One moment. I want from you, Amazon, the whereabouts of your Ultra in the first Galaxy. If war comes here following the destruction of the Pagan cities I shall make it my business to escape into space and claim your space ship Ultra for myself. I have a detector here, but without the magnetism factor of the Ultra—which can only be found normally by months of work, as Milford found it—I shall be unreasonably delayed in my escape. What is that factor?"

The Amazon smiled contemptuously, a glitter of defiance in her violet eyes.

"I am waiting," Karg said, leveling his weapon more directly. The Amazon did not attempt further defiance, realizing as she did that Karg would use the gun with devastating effect on her if he lost his temper.

"Whether the scale reading on your detector corresponds with mine I do not know," she said, "but it is 4670—"

"That is all I wish to know. I can work out the equivalent difference if need be, just as long as I have the basic figure." Karg used his free hand to drag a notebook out of his uniform, then still covering the Amazon he put the book down on the bench and felt again for his pen. He found it, wrote down the number, and returned the book to his pocket. But returning the pen was not so simple. It jammed somewhere in the lining, and for a second, Karg glanced down at the difficulty. Instantly the Amazon seized her chance, catapulting forward and delivering a smashing uppercut at the same time. Karg flew backwards helplessly and clutched at the bench to save himself falling. He shook his head violently and then straightened as the proton gun was snatched from his hand and leveled at him. The Amazon was smiling slightly; but Karg was under no illusion concerning the hard look in her violet eyes.

"Just one small slip, my friend," she commented. "And you have only your pen to thank for it. We're alone, as you have good reason to know, and you have lost the initiative. You certainly won't regain it. On the contrary, you are going to put in some useful work. You are going to agree to General Milford's ultimatum."

"You'll never make me do that," Karg snapped back.

"No?" The Amazon laughed softly. "I'll give you a choice, Karg. Either do that, speaking the words I'll dictate to you, or else I shall inflict untold suffering on you until you do." The Amazon shrugged. "And don't think I wouldn't do it either. As a tigress plays with her victim, so I'll play with you—unless you see sense."

Karg jumped and then sweated visibly as the proton gun abruptly fired and left a smoking hole in the bench not an inch from his supporting hand. The Amazon chuckled softly.

"You called me a she-devil," she said icily. "How right you were..." The gun jerked upwards. "Well, which is it to be?"

"I'll—I'll do as you say," Karg panted, knowing he was cornered, and not doubting in the least that this fantastic woman would make good her threat if she had to.

"Switch on the radio," the Amazon commanded. Then when Karg had done so, "Instead of me giving orders to the robots as you had intended, Karg, you will give release to your people. I shall speak in a low voice and you will repeat my words exactly... First, make your radio call especially applicable to General Milford. Calling General Milford—" The Amazon lounged in relentless attention by the bench and then continued: "Calling General Milford— or if he is not immediately available transmit this message to him. I, Karg of the Pagans, herewith accept the ultimatum given by General Milford and I agree to his suggestion that a world plebiscite be held in which the peoples of both Normal and Pagan communities can decide for themselves which government they prefer..."

The Amazon paused and, with obvious reluctance in his voice, Karg repeated her words slowly into the microphone. She listened to the monitor speaker and surveyed the output meters to be sure the broadcast was going forth, and then continued:

"I, as leader of the Pagans, hereby undertake to release from my rulership all those who wish to depart, and no reprisal will be taken—"

Karg hesitated, aware he was swearing away all his power. Then he looked up as the gun jammed suddenly in his ribs and smoldering purple eyes looked fixedly into his. The Amazon's voice came with steely softness: "Do it! Speak!"

Karg still hesitated, then finally the unwavering gun decided him. This was a position in which he could not argue. He spoke the words, then when he had finished, all the fight seemed to go out of him. He relaxed limply against the bench, fingering his still throbbing jaw.

"Very sensible of you," the Amazon commented, "You cannot retract now you have broadcast a promise, and to make doubly sure that you don't I shall give orders to the Mercutian robots to be constantly in readiness with the lens. And remember, they live on eternally, always ready, far out-stripping your own lifetime, my friend."

This last taunt was too much and it spurred Karg to sudden and violent action, so much so the Amazon never expected it from his relaxed pose. He lashed out his hand and knocked the proton gun out of her grasp, snatching it from the floor before she had a chance to retrieve it. The Amazon waited, furious with herself, ready for the gun blast that she knew would finish her. The blast came—but it was only a needle-thin shaft of flame that missed the Amazon by inches. Then she remembered; she had not changed the nozzle focus from when she had blasted the bench. Easy enough for her to handle, but not for the unaccustomed Karg. He swore and fired again, but by this time the Amazon had vaulted to shelter behind one of the many tall metal instrument cabinets.

Karg fired again, but behind the cabinet the Amazon had complete safety—as long as the gun were on the narrow beam, where it was likely to remain since Karg did not understand how to alter it—nor was their time for investigation. Finally, another plan evidently in his mind, he flung back the bolts of the door and vanished in the corridor…

For several seconds the Amazon waited for something to happen, then as nothing did she cautiously emerged from her shelter and looked about her. A moment afterwards Abna came in, puzzled and curious. Relief crossed his face as he saw the Amazon.

"What happened?" he demanded. "Karg got away from us. We couldn't do anything else with a proton gun fixed on us—"

The Amazon relaxed slowly. "Let him go, Abna; we've got the position well in hand and he daren't come back…" Briefly she related the details. "A pretty near thing, too, if that gun hadn't been on the micro nozzle I'd have been finished. Evidently there were too many of you in the corridor for him to risk the consequences of firing at any one of you. We'd better get away from here and let Milford know how the situation stands. Doubtless he'll know already but he'll want our point of view."

* * * *

Milford certainly knew the facts; he had heard them all over the radio, and so for that matter had all the people of both Normal and Pagan communities. The shifting and changing had already begun as unwilling Pagans packed up their belongings and prepared to transfer themselves to the nearest Normal community. And so the process would continue until finally the Normals were in such a majority there could be no doubt as to the outcome of the potential plebiscite.

"And you, my friends, we cannot thank enough," Milford said quietly, when he and the Amazon were at the end of their respective stories and the dawn light was coming through the windows. "Thanks to what you have done, and the legacy of the robots waiting on Mercury and always near the lens, there can be no doubt as to the future. That lens is a guarantee of peace on Earth for many generations to come. You have done a job well—wonderfully well."

"We've done our best," the Amazon smiled, rising. "There is only one thing that disturbs me. Karg is not dead—and he will take care to remain free. Presumably he has fled somewhere from the possible wrath of those he dominated—but to *where* has he fled?"

"Does that matter so much?" Milford questioned. "He'll never get control again—or even dare to show his face. I repeat—the lens is our guarantee of immunity."

The Amazon did not seem to be listening. There was that faraway look in her eyes. Abna and the others waited expectantly—and in a moment it came. The Amazon asked a question as she turned back to Milford.

"You have hyperspatial radar equipment and, you say, a detector with which you found the Ultra's position?"

"Most certainly. As far as the detector is concerned, it has never been altered and must be focused on your spaceship in the First Galaxy. But what has this to do with Karg?"

"Possibly everything," the Amazon replied grimly. "I would like to examine both radar equipment and detector right away."

The request was no sooner made than granted, and for a long time the Amazon stood in the great Lexicon testing laboratory, the others including Milford around her, as she examined the scanning screen of the radar equipment—focused directly on the spatial course out of the Solar System which led toward the Milky Way. And the scanner was picking something up—a small, moving object traveling at high velocity.

Then, apparently satisfied but not saying anything, the Amazon turned her attention to the detector and looked at the number on the graded scale opposite to the delicately quivering, immensely sensitive needle.

"So as yet the Ultra is still there," she said, musing. "No space marauder has attempted to steal it."

"There for you to take up again whenever you wish," Milford smiled. "We will give you every facility as we promised. The fastest of our space machines—"

"The faster the better," the Amazon nodded grimly. "If we don't get to the Ultra with all possible speed, then Karg certainly will. He is already halfway out of the Solar System."

"He's what!" Milford looked his surprise, and Abna, Viona, Mexone and Thania glanced at each other.

"There's your proof," the Amazon said, nodding to the radar scanner. "There is an object there moving with great speed, something small and solid, and the distance away it is, it can only be a space ship... Definitely it is Karg. That's what he did when he left Railstrom, took the first space ship he could find and hurtled into space."

"But why in the direction of the Ultra?" Viona demanded. "He can't possibly know where to find it."

"Unhappily, he can." The Amazon looked grim. "He took an object compass bearing when he had the whip hand over me, and I was forced to give it him or risk the proton gun. He'll be able to work out the bearing from the detector he must have aboard his space ship."

There was silence for a moment, then Abna said:

"At all costs he mustn't get there first. With the weapons there are aboard the Ultra he could come back and make things tougher than they ever were. The Zero thought amplifier alone could give him that mastery."

"I know it." The Amazon turned sharply. "We've got to act fast. My work is done here, General Milford. Please make arrangements for the two fastest space ships you've got to be placed immediately at our disposal—and make sure one of them is well armed. Abna and I will take the armed ship—" the Amazon glanced at Viona and the others—"and you three will take the other ship. Your job will be to head straight for the Ultra and secure it. Abna and I will deal with Karg." She hurried toward the door.

"Quickly, the rest of you. We'll give ourselves an hour, and no longer, to get ready. Then we're off—to stop Karg even if we burn out our atomic motors in the process. We must reach the Ultra, the Zero thought machine, before he does!"

MORE BORGO PRESS TITLES BY JOHN RUSSELL FEARN

THE ADAM QUIRKE SERIES

The Master Must Die: A Science Fiction Mystery
The Lonely Astronomer : A Science Fiction Mystery

THE ANJANI SERIES

The Gold of Akada: A Jungle Adventure Novel
Anjani the Mighty: A Lost Race Novel

THE BLACK MARIA SERIES

Black Maria, M.A.: A Classic Crime Novel
The Murdered Schoolgirl: A Classic Crime Novel
One Remained Seated: A Classic Crime Novel
Thy Arm Alone: A Classic Crime Novel
Death in Silhouette: A Classic Crime Novel

THE HERBERT THE DINOSAUR SERIES

A Thing of the Past
The Genial Dinosaur

OTHER BOOKS

1,000-Year Voyage: A Science Fiction Novel
Account Settled: A Science Fiction Mystery

Before Earth Came: Classic Science Fiction Stories
Bury the Hatchet: A Crime Tale
A Case for Brutus Lloyd: A Science Fiction Mystery
The Crimson Rambler: A Crime Novel
Don't Touch Me: A Crime Novel
Dynasty of the Small: Classic Science Fiction Stories
The Empty Coffins: A Mystery of Horror
The Fourth Door: A Mystery Novel
From Afar: A Science Fiction Mystery
Fugitive of Time: A Classic Science Fiction Novel
The G-Bomb: A Science Fiction Novel
The Haunted Gallery: Crime Stories
Here and Now: A Science Fiction Novel
Into the Unknown: A Science Fiction Tale
Last Conflict: Classic Science Fiction Stories
Legacy from Sirius: A Classic Science Fiction Novel
The Man from Hell: Classic Science Fiction Stories
The Man Who Was Not: A Crime Novel
Manton's World: A Classic Science Fiction Novel
Moon Magic: A Novel of Romance (as Elizabeth Rutland)
One Way Out: A Crime Novel (with Philip Harbottle)
Pattern of Murder: A Classic Crime Novel
Reflected Glory: A Dr. Castle Classic Crime Novel
Robbery Without Violence: Two Science Fiction Crime Stories
Rule of the Brains: Classic Science Fiction Stories
Shattering Glass: A Crime Novel
The Silvered Cage: A Scientific Murder Mystery
Slaves of Ijax: A Science Fiction Novel
Something from Mercury: Classic Science Fiction Stories
The Space Warp: A Science Fiction Novel
The Time Trap: A Science Fiction Novel
Valley of Pretenders: Classic Science Fiction Stories
Vision Sinister: A Scientific Detective Thriller
Voice of the Conqueror: A Classic Science Fiction Novel
What Happened to Hammond? A Scientific Mystery
Within That Room!: A Classic Crime Novel
World Without Chance: Classic Science Fiction Stories